Donated by
Floyd Dickman

Funerals & Fly Fishing

Funerals & Fly Fishing

MARY BARTEK

Henry Holt and Company
New York

I'd like to gratefully acknowledge several people who helped make this book possible: the current and past members of the Tuesday Night Writer's Group, especially those who helped develop this book through its infancy: Boni Hamilton, Roxana Chalmers, Lynn Kinghorn, Jennie Shortridge, and Carol Bryant; my father, Hugh Marron, who in his lifetime was a good man and a well-respected funeral director; my husband, Robert Bartek, who contributed his expertise in fly fishing and his support for my writing life; my daughters and extended family who have always had confidence in my efforts; Alison Picard, my agent, and Christy Ottaviano, my editor, both of whom offered excellent editorial guidance; and my students who supported this book, some by offering to read it and many by providing inspiration.

Henry Holt and Company, LLC
Publishers since 1866
115 West 18th Street
New York, New York 10011
www.henryholt.com

Henry Holt is a registered trademark of Henry Holt and Company, LLC
Copyright © 2004 by Mary Bartek
Distributed in Canada by H. B. Fenn and Company Ltd.

Library of Congress Cataloging-in-Publication Data
Bartek, Mary.
Funerals and fly fishing / Mary Bartek—1st ed.
p.   cm.
Summary: The summer after sixth grade, Brad Stanislawski travels to
Pennsylvania by himself to visit the grandfather he has never met
before, and overcomes some of the preconceived ideas he has gotten
from his mother.
ISBN 0-8050-7409-0
EAN 978-0-8050-7409-0
[1. Grandfathers—Fiction. 2. Undertakers and undertaking—Fiction.
3. Family—Fiction. 4. Pennsylvania—Fiction.] I. Title.
PZ7.B28066Fu 2004
[Fic]—dc22   2003057046

First edition—2004
Printed in the United States of America on acid-free paper. ∞

1   3   5   7   9   10   8   6   4   2

For my mother, Stella Marron,
who always knew I was a writer

Funerals & Fly Fishing

1

The Last Day of School

"Brad? Brad Stanislawski? Did you hear me?"

My pencil freezes mid-doodle. The art teacher's voice jerks me back to reality. I must have missed the beginning of this conversation. She looks annoyed, and the kids around me are snickering.

"I said I'd like all students to claim their work if it's still on display." She looks at the almost-bare art room walls. "Yours are the only pictures still affixed."

"You can have them, Mrs. Avery," I say quietly. "I don't need them."

"Thoughtful of you though that is, Mr. Stanislawski, I don't need them either." More snickers from around the room. "Would you remove them, please?"

"Sure." I get up. My chair slides back too far and clunks into the seat behind me. Rachel Martin, a tiny girl with a loud mouth, lets out a sigh that's noisier than my chair.

I am so glad it's the last day of sixth grade that Mrs. Avery's attitude hardly even bothers me. Usually when I go to a new school, the art teacher is the one person who makes me feel like I belong there. Mrs. Avery has been the exception. She likes my drawings well enough to keep putting them up, but I seem to annoy her just by being in the room. On the day I arrived three months ago, the first words out of her mouth were "I don't have an extra desk. I don't know where I'm going to put you," followed closely by "Stan— Stanis— How do you say your name?"

So now I stand beside my desk without moving. I'm trying to plan the route to the walls that will cause me the least trouble. Just my luck, the two biggest creeps in the class don't sit together here like they do everywhere else. Mrs. Avery never lets troublemakers sit side by side. It makes it easier for her to keep them under control, I guess, but at the moment it's severely limiting my options: I can't get to the walls without passing directly by either Jason Miller or Anthony DeVito.

"Mr. Stanislawski?" Mrs. Avery says. "Do you need help finding your seat?"

By the class's reaction, she could have a great future at the Comedy Club. Maybe now that she's retiring, stand-up comedy will be her next gig.

I don't bother answering. I start for the pictures.

Unfortunately, since my eyes were checking out how I could avoid Jason and my feet were already planning to stay away from Anthony, I trip on my first step. I saved both of them the trouble this time. They should thank me.

Overall, sixth grade has not been my favorite. Not at North Middle in Denver, where I started the year, and not here on the southern edge of the Denver suburbs. Just as she has with every other move, my mom keeps saying, "Look at all the people you're getting to meet. I never had those opportunities." When I mention that no one seems especially interested in meeting me, she says, "Just look for the friendly faces." Apparently, this is the year when all the friendly kids moved out the week before I moved in.

My mom used to work as a receptionist at a real estate office that also handled rental properties. Whenever Mom heard about a decent place for less rent than we were paying, she'd start packing boxes. She got her agent's license a while back, and this time when she found a great deal she bought the house instead of renting it. That could mean we're staying put, but I'm not counting on it.

This is also the year I grew four and a half inches, something I am reminded of on the weekdays when I hear somebody refer to me as "that big kid," and on the weekends when my mom says, "I wish I could know how much taller you're going to get before we invest in clothes again." She always smiles after she says that, but it makes me feel guilty anyway. I'd quit growing if I could figure out how.

I take my time getting my four drawings off the walls, and Mrs. Avery seems to have forgotten about me. She's droning on to the class about how she hopes they have a good summer vacation. She looks at the clock, talks, looks at the clock again. I know how much I want the next two class periods to fly by, so I can sympathize with Mrs. Avery. She must be ready to go nuts, stuck in this room for the last thirty years.

I pull the last drawing off the wall and start back between the rows of desks just as the bell rings. Suddenly, I'm on a one-way street, driving the wrong way. The kids behind me are blocking the retreat, and I can't move forward either. Worst of all, I'm nose to nose with Jason. "Get out of my way, you ox," he growls, well within earshot of Mrs. Avery.

"Mr. Miller," she bellows, "I heard that."

"I didn't mean you, Mrs. Avery," he says. I knew this guy was stupid, but that last line verges on a death wish.

"Sit, Mr. Miller," she says, pointing as if he were her dog, "and don't get up until I tell you to."

This time the snickers are aimed at Jason. I try not to look at him, but his squinty glare drags my eyes like a magnet.

"Later, Stanislawski," he says, just loud enough for me to hear.

2

Problems and Prizes

I waste no time leaving the building after the last bell. Not that I have any great plans for summer. It's just that right now *not* going to school every day for the next ten weeks sounds like vacation enough.

Hopping on my bike, I can't help smiling. I start toward home feeling like everyone who sees me will automatically think the word *freedom*. This is my best day since we moved.

My great mood lasts for a record three and one-half blocks, when somewhere close behind me a water balloon hits the sidewalk. It lets out a loud *whoosh*, but just a few drops splash my leg. I keep pedaling.

"Hey, Brad-lee, wait up!" Jason whines my first name in a loud, obnoxious voice. I know that will be Anthony's cue to murder my last name.

"Get back here, Stan-is-lousy!" he yells.

For the millionth time, I promise myself that the

first thing I'll do when I'm eighteen is change my name. But I don't have a chance to sit around thinking about it now. I pedal faster. Unfortunately, so do Jason and Anthony.

I still have a couple of bike lengths on them. I'm taller than these Neanderthals, but I've got more than a few pounds on them, too. Out-biking them isn't easy. The burning in the back of my calf is about to turn into a full-blown muscle-twister.

Another water balloon whooshes. This one lands even with my back tire, but off to the left. I get a wet ankle out of it.

Time for Plan B. There's a cul-de-sac just around the curve. I hope I know this neighborhood better than these jerks do. At the last possible second I veer into the little street pocket and up between two houses where I know there's a shortcut. Gravel sprays behind me as they try to follow, but somebody's bike goes down. Judging from the swearing, I'm guessing it's Anthony's.

"I'll get you, Stan-is-lousy!" Yep, it's definitely Anthony's, but I don't turn around. I just remind myself that sixth grade is finally over. I concentrate on feeling the breeze dry my sweaty hair as I finish the ride home.

Walking into the house, I let the screen door slam behind me. When my mom doesn't yell at me for it, I realize she's on the phone. I walk into the kitchen to grab a snack.

Mom is sitting at the kitchen table with the phone in her hand. Her voice sounds calm, but it doesn't match her face. She looks upset.

"I understand, really. . . . It's not like you have any choice." There's a pause, and then she adds, "Don't give it another thought. I'll work something out. Bye now." She sets the phone on the table, then lets her head klunk down beside it. Tea sloshes in the mug beside her. A few drops spill out.

Assuming that she'll tell me what's the matter when she's ready, I put down my backpack, pour myself a glass of milk, and grab a couple of cookies. I carry the snack to the table and sit down across from her. I'm halfway through the first cookie when she slowly sits up.

"Bad day?" I ask.

Mom's eyes widen. "Oh, I've had better. That was Laura on the phone. Her sister in Nebraska—the one with the two-year-old twins and the husband in the Army—broke her leg yesterday. She's begging Laura to come up and help her. She says she doesn't have anyone else to ask. So Laura's family is leaving tonight."

Laura is my mom's best friend. We've known her forever. She lives on the other side of town, near where Mom lived when I was a baby. She and her husband have a four-year-old named Nathan who's a pretty cute kid.

"Is she going to be back before you leave for California?"

Mom lets out a sigh and answers, "I don't see how she could be."

I'm supposed to stay with Laura's family while my mom goes on vacation. It's not the kind of thing Mom has done before—ever—but this has been planned for months. After working long hours all last winter at the real estate office, she earned the Rookie of the Year Award. Among the new hires she sold the most properties. Not the expensive ones with the high commissions. But at least there were a lot of them, and that's what counted. As a bonus, the company gave her the trip.

Mom runs a hand through her hair, stands up, and says, "I've got a house to show. I'll have to worry about this later."

She grabs her keys and purse, then turns back to me. "I'm sorry, honey. I didn't even ask you how the last day of school went."

I wave her on.

"It was fine. It's summer vacation now. How bad can that be?"

"Great." She continues toward the door. "I shouldn't be long, okay?"

"Sure. See you later."

I pull out my sketchbook and pencil and take it to the back porch with the rest of my milk. Propping myself against the porch railing, I put pencil to paper.

"I had another swell day, Mom," I say to no one. My pencil takes off and wants to draw something ugly. It's a monster that's more apelike than anything, but its eyes bulge in a disgusting, bloodshot way. "I get to spend my days with people who either ignore me . . ." The monster is hunched over the handlebars of a bike that's two sizes too small for him. The hair on his back twists into little curlicues. ". . . or they have nothing better to do than make fun of my last name."

The monster has buckteeth. I'd make them yellow, but this is a pencil sketch, so some shading will have to do. I check out what I've drawn so far, trying to decide what's missing. A minute later, I'm putting the finishing touches on Anthony's baseball cap. It looks perfect on the monster's head.

I draw Jason and Anthony in as many bug-eyed, scaly ways as I can think of, and still Mom's not back.

Suddenly, I realize that I've got an answer for her vacation problem: I'll go with her. I tossed out that suggestion when she first told me about earning the trip. She had a bunch of reasons why it couldn't work at the time. But if she wants to go, she'll *have* to take me. I know she's not going to let me stay home alone.

I put away the sketchbook and get out a sheet of paper. "See It This Summer," I write at the top, and start my list:

1. The Pacific Ocean,
2. Disneyland,
3. A Disney animator,
4. A movie star,
5. Palm trees.

I know my list will get a lot longer before the trip, so I number the rest of the way down the page to fill in later.

The truth is, there are about a million things I could write on this list. All I've ever really seen is Denver—North Denver, South Denver, East Denver. Everybody's been more places than I have.

I've taken three phone messages by the time Mom comes in at about six-thirty, and the first thing I do is hand them to her. Real estate agents get called a lot, so I've become a good message-taker. This time, though, she doesn't even look at them. Instead, she sits down on the step beside me, pulls out a cigarette, and fumbles around for a while as she tries to light it. She takes a couple of puffs and says, "Okay, kiddo, I've got a new plan."

3

A Change of Plans

"Here's the deal," Mom says. "I think I've come up with a way that I can still go on the trip." She takes another puff on her cigarette. "But I'll need your help."

I think she wants to surprise me, but I can't keep from smiling.

"You've decided to take me with you!" I look at her, expecting to see her face break into a grin like mine. Instead, she wrinkles her forehead and starts shaking her head.

"Brad, we already discussed that, remember? I can't afford to take you. To be honest, even if I could this wouldn't be the right time." She sighed. "I really need to get away by myself for a bit."

The smile slides off my face. Stumped for any other possibilities, I ask, "Do you want me to stay here alone?" That option does sound sort of interesting. "I guess I could do that."

"Of course not."

As far as I can see, we're at the bottom of the choice list. "Then what?"

"I've had time to give it some thought on the drive home. I tried to picture what else we could do. I couldn't think of any friends you have from school that you might want to stay with. Can you?"

She's got to be kidding. "Stay with? There's no one from school that I even want to talk to."

She raises her eyebrows but doesn't stay distracted for long. "Anyway, it finally occurred to me that there might be one other possibility. Your grandfather wrote again recently, suggesting you come and see him. So"— she takes a deep breath before she rushes through the rest of her sentence—"I'm thinking you and I could take vacations at the same time."

"You want me to visit your father? I don't even know him. He's someone who sends me a birthday card— that's it."

"I'm just offering it as an option. You could go to Pennsylvania while I go to California."

When I don't say anything, she keeps talking.

"He's even offered to pay your way, so I was thinking that could be a good solution. How about it?" She smiles, I guess to pretend that this is a fun idea.

My mom and I usually get along pretty well. It's always

been just the two of us. But when I hear her say "a good solution," both my hands clench into fists.

"You need a solution to your problem, and *I'm* the problem, is that it?"

"Brad, no."

"Too bad there aren't any kennels where you can send me. Anyplace with food and water would be just fine." The sarcasm pours out of me.

"You're not being fair," she says.

"*I'm* not being fair?" My voice keeps getting louder, but I don't seem to be able to stop it. "You get to go to the beach, and I have to stay with some old person I don't even know?"

"I'm sorry," she says. "I don't know what else to do."

Mom had been looking out at the grass. When she finally looks at me, I'm afraid she's going to start crying. I try to ignore it.

"You could wait, and we could go some other time," I say.

"And when would that be? I've been trying to win a bonus for as long as I've had my license." Now she *is* crying, which is pretty impossible to ignore. "Who knows when I'll be able to pull it off again?"

I want to keep arguing, but I've run out of ammunition. What am I going to do? Keep her from going to California?

"Okay, I'll go," I say finally. "But I don't have to like it. As far as I'm concerned, this is just some guy who got stuck baby-sitting me."

And so, just days after that conversation, I'm boarding a U.S. Airways flight to Pittsburgh, ready to travel fifteen hundred miles to meet a stranger.

1

The Trip

I'm sure Mom wishes she could hang a six-inch tag from my neck saying "I'm Brad Stanislawski. If I get lost please return me to . . ." After she smothers me with enough hugs and kisses to last until I'm twenty, she has to settle for whispering to the flight attendant as I get on the plane. "My son is twelve. He's flying alone, and this is his first flight," she says. "Please keep an eye on him."

All morning she's been telling me she'll miss me, but I'm guessing she'll be relieved when the plane actually takes off. Mom had already locked in the plans for me to go to Pennsylvania when I started bugging her about why my grandfather has never come to see us, or why we haven't gone to see him, for that matter. "I remember you used to say he was too busy. But nobody's that busy. What's the deal?"

She opened her mouth to say something, but nothing

came out. It was like I had just asked some trick question that caught her off guard.

"Well," she said, "we don't really talk to each other." Then, she added, as if it explained everything, "So we don't visit."

"You mean I'm going to stay with someone that you won't even talk to?"

"That would be true," she said. "But it doesn't mean you won't talk to him."

I sat down on the couch, crossed my arms in front of me, and used the parent voice I learned from her to say, "Explain, please."

"You're right," she said. "I guess you do deserve an explanation, especially after all this time."

So she finally spilled the story about her move to Colorado.

"My dad and I never did get along too well," she said. "But our differences were no worse than most fathers and daughters have, I think, until I started dating your dad." She let out a laugh that seemed to come through her nose. "My father didn't like Brad Parsons, not one bit. He forbade me to see him. But we had already fallen in love, and nothing my father said was going to make any difference. So as soon as we graduated, Brad and I took off for Colorado."

"And before you could get married, that's when he

got killed in the car accident?" I asked. That's the only part of the story my mom had ever told me. She could have given me my dad's last name when I was born, but she thought having my name match hers made more sense.

"Yes," she said. "When Brad died, that was the worst. If I hadn't been so hurt and angry, I guess I would have turned around and gone home. But somehow I felt I'd be turning my back on your dad if I did. I kept in touch with my mom occasionally by phone. She actually came out here once for a few days right after you were born. But it wasn't something she could afford to do all the time. And, of course, I doubt that my father approved."

"So you've never been back to Pennsylvania?" I asked.

"Only for a few days when Mom died. I guess you're too young to remember that."

She had been talking so calmly that I almost forgot what a rotten thing she was doing to me, sending me where even she wouldn't go.

"So now I'm supposed to stay with a man that you don't like?" I asked when she was finished.

"The differences were ours, not yours, Brad," Mom said. "As I told you, I've had some notes from him in the last few months. He's asked to meet you. I'm sure he'll be kind."

"And if we let him meet me, you get to go to California."

"Guilty as charged," Mom said. At least she was honest about it.

The brown-haired flight attendant is treating me like a two-year-old, but I smile at her anyway. "Brad, I hope you enjoy your flight. My name is Sarah. Let me know if there's anything you need." With any luck, being on her good side will get me an extra soda or two. Now that I've agreed to do this, I might as well enjoy it. I buckle my seat belt, ready to log my first air miles, draw clouds up close, and eat pretzels.

The takeoff isn't too scary, and by the time I open my eyes the world looks peaceful out the airplane window. It's a three-hour flight, but it doesn't feel that long. After the flight attendants serve everybody snacks and then clean up, the pilot tells us we're flying over Cleveland.

I pull out the photograph my mom gave me last night. "It's about ten years old, I guess. This was my mom," she told me, pointing to a short, curly-haired woman. "This is your grandfather." I took the picture from her to get a better look.

Examining it again, I can't tell much more than I could last night. His hair is brown like mine. The picture isn't a close-up, but he looks friendly enough. Of course, he could be a mean person who's just smiling for the camera.

The flight attendant's voice comes over the loudspeaker. "We are starting our descent. Please return your seats to their upright positions." I zip my grandfather's picture into my backpack pocket.

My stomach isn't too crazy about the plane landing. When we finally touch down in Pittsburgh, I'm holding the barf bag just in case. Luckily, my stomach lands a minute after the plane does.

Sarah helps me grab my stuff. "Did you enjoy the flight?"

I don't trust everything to stay inside if I open my mouth, so I simply smile and nod like an idiot. I hook my backpack over my shoulder and start down the aisle.

"Brad, over here." My grandfather calls to me the minute I step into the waiting area. I guess my mom must have sent him a picture, too.

He looks like he did in the picture, except that his hair is more gray than brown now, and his stomach might have grown a little. Also, he's taller than I thought he would be. Maybe my grandmother wasn't so short after all. Maybe it was standing next to him that made her look that way.

He shakes my hand. "Good to have you here, boy."

Did he just call me boy?

"Shall we get your bags? I need to get on back to the funeral home."

Funeral home? Mom told me that her family used to live above one, but surely he doesn't still, does he?

I glance out the airport window to the plane I've just gotten off. It's all I can do not to run and beg to get back on.

5

The Stanislawski Funeral Home

My grandfather and I head over to the baggage claim area. We stand side by side, staring up into the chute where the bags will eventually pop out.

"Would you like to use the restroom? I'm sure there's one nearby," he says.

"No, thanks. I went on the plane."

We're quiet again, and a minute later he says, "So you used the restroom on the airplane?"

"Yes," I say. "It's really small." Then I add, "The drains sound like they're sucking the water into space, and the faucet handles are tiny."

"That's true," he answers. We seem to be done talking again.

Pretty soon the luggage machine buzzes to warn us that the bags are coming. All the people crowd in to get their suitcases. I've brought two duffel bags. The first one shows up right away, but my grandfather is checking his watch a lot by the time we get the second one. We each carry a bag to the parking lot.

Since he knows where the car is, I drop back a step and follow in his shadow. He casts a huge one. I challenge myself to stay inside the gray edges as we walk. It takes some fancy footwork. I'm doing great until my grandfather suddenly stops, and I plow into him. My duffel almost chops him at the knees.

"Sorry," I say, bouncing off.

He just looks down at me and nods, taking the duffel from me. "This is the car," he says, pressing a button on his key chain that unlocks the doors and pops the trunk. The car is black, shiny, and expensive-looking. It's nothing like ours. There's not a fast food napkin or a Coke can in sight. I guess it's his business car. I'm just glad it's not a hearse.

"It will take us about two hours to get home," he says. He switches on the radio to some station where the music all sounds bouncy but there aren't any words.

Since my grandfather doesn't seem to be a talker, it's easy just to stare out at the trees. And are there a lot of them! We pass more trees in the first five miles from the airport than I've seen in the whole state of Colorado. It's a sunny day, but the branches are so thick overhead that sometimes they block the sun completely.

"So, how do you like Colorado?" my grandfather asks.

"It's fine. We don't have so many big trees there," I say.

"Your mother always talked about going out West."

I almost say, "You know my mom?" Then I remember that he's her dad, and that weird thought makes me run out of conversation again. I wish we had saved our discussion of airplane bathrooms for the car.

I don't remember falling asleep, but somehow I'm waking up as we pull to a stop. We're in front of a huge white house with a sign that says STANISLAWSKI FUNERAL HOME in big letters and has STANLEY STANISLAWSKI, PROPRIETOR written smaller underneath. My grandfather's name is Stanley? And I thought I had it bad.

"We're here." He gets out of the car, heads right up to the main entrance, and pulls the door open for me. Obviously, I'm supposed to go inside but I don't want to walk in on any dead people. I guess he understands why I'm hesitating because he says, "There's no viewing today. It's okay to go in this way."

It's cool in the entryway and a little dark. I can see into the wide rooms on each side of the hallway, and I decide I'm not moving any farther. There are open caskets lining the walls. Double curtains cover all the windows, heavy ones that are open, and filmy ones underneath that are closed.

My grandfather puts his hand around a corner and flips on a light switch. As soon as he does, a much younger guy in jeans and a hospital-worker kind of shirt appears at the end of the hall.

"Well, Stanley," the man says, smiling and walking toward us, "this must be your grandson."

"Yes," my grandfather answers. "Mike, this is Brad."

Mike shakes my hand. "Nice to meet you. Your grandfather has sure been looking forward to your visit."

I look up at my grandfather and see that he doesn't look too pleased at the moment. "Are you working downstairs?" he asks Mike.

"Yes. We got a call just after you left. Walter Chihoski died at the hospital. I'm almost finished."

"I wish you had paged me," my grandfather says, sounding annoyed. "What time is the family coming in to select a casket?"

Mike looks at his watch. "Gee," he says, looking surprised, "in about fifteen minutes. I'd better get changed."

"No," my grandfather says. "I'll take care of it. You finish with Mr. Chihoski. Brad," he says, turning to me, "let's take your bags upstairs, then I have to meet with some people."

"See you later," Mike says, heading back the way he came.

"Bye," I say.

My grandfather leads the way up the stairs and opens a door at the top. Before I look in, my eyes clamp shut on their own. A chill runs up one of my arms and down the other. I've been here all of five minutes, and I've already seen a dozen open caskets. Not only that, but I have a bad feeling that there's a dead guy in here somewhere. Who knows what surprises my grandfather keeps upstairs?

6

Wallace Corners, Pennsylvania

"Come on in and make yourself at home," my grandfather says. He steps through the doorway, turns around, and waits for me to follow.

I take a deep breath, then walk in. I can hardly believe what I see. The room we enter is nothing like I expected because it's so normal. Completely, entirely normal. It's just a living room. Couch, two chairs, two end tables with lamps on them, TV with a VCR. The sun coming through the window makes a big patch of light on the beige carpet, and there's a cat curled up on the sunny spot. She opens her eyes when we come in, but closes them again. Since the windows are open, the curtains are floating up and down on the breeze. It looks just like anybody's house.

"Let's go," my grandfather says. "I'll show you to your room."

We pass a dining room and kitchen on the right as we walk down a long hallway. There are two other doors on the way to the one where he puts my things.

"This was your mom's room," he says. "It's still a bit girlish. I hope you don't mind."

There's a double bed, some bookshelves, and a desk so neat that it's obvious no one really lives here anymore. Except for the teddy bear sitting on the bed and the blue flowers all over the bedspread, it's okay. "It's fine," I tell him. "Blue is still my mom's favorite color." As I say that, she pops into my head. I wonder if she's gotten to California yet. I also wonder if she's feeling rotten for sending me to a funeral home.

As if to give me proof that my mother was really here once, there's a picture of my grandparents with her standing between them. I'll have to take a better look at it later. Even from across the room, I can tell that those glasses and that hairdo are going to be something I can tease her about for a long time.

"Come on out in the kitchen for a minute," my grandfather says, leading the way. He opens the refrigerator door. "There's some Coke and 7 UP in here. I didn't know what you'd like."

I catch a peek in the refrigerator as he closes the door. Before he added the soda, there wasn't much else. Just milk, ketchup, and jelly, by the look of things.

He swings open the freezer door. "What I mostly have is bachelor food." The freezer is stacked with frozen dinner boxes, as if he emptied that one whole section at the grocery store. He closes the door, reaches into his pants pocket for his wallet, and pulls out a twenty-dollar bill. "If you wouldn't mind," he says, "I'd appreciate it if you'd go down to the store to pick up some bread, some lunch meat that you'd like, and whatever else you think we ought to have."

The words "Who was your slave yesterday?" come to mind, but I don't say them. Instead I just ask, "I should walk?"

"Yes, if you would. It's not too far." He tells me how to get there, and I'm glad to hear there are no turns involved. I really don't feel like getting lost on my first day in Wallace Corners.

"Sure," I say. "No problem." It's not like I have a lot of options for entertainment in a funeral home. Plus, I'll be able to add "grocery store" to my See It This Summer list.

"I'll finish my work downstairs, we can have a little supper, and then I thought we could take in a baseball game tonight."

"Okay, I'll see you soon."

A minute later, he's gone.

I'm not a major sports fanatic, but seeing the Pittsburgh Pirates should be cool. This might not be a totally wasted trip after all.

I head down the street in the direction that my grand-father told me. His big, white funeral home seems to be the fanciest house in the neighborhood. The houses here aren't junky-looking, just small and old. Where I live, there's a new housing development or a new school being built all the time. From what I can tell, they finished building Wallace Corners when my grandfather was a kid and didn't make many changes after that.

The closer I get to the store, the more businesses there are: a dry cleaner, a flower shop, a bank, a movie theater. The street looks familiar and I finally remember why. It's like the all-American '50s town in my favorite movie, *Back to the Future*. The only difference is that there doesn't seem to be a square in the middle of town, plus the clock tower here is on top of the church—that is, on one of the churches. There are lots of them.

When I get to the grocery store, I grab the bread and lunch meat like he asked me to. I'm not sure what else to buy. I don't want my grandfather to think that what he has isn't good enough. Besides, his frozen dinners look fine to me. Mom doesn't have those very often. She says she prefers "real food." With all her appointments to show houses, though, we end up eating fast food half the time. I finally pick out a container of orange juice, a frozen pizza, and some Oreos.

The cashier seems to know everyone in the checkout line. She works pretty fast, even though she's got a conversation going with all the shoppers who come through. When it's my turn, she looks as if she's going to say something friendly, then settles for "Did you find everything all right?" I just smile and nod.

As I leave the store, I hear somebody yell, "Hey, dopeface!"

I jerk my head up, and the hair on the back of my neck tingles. I'm ready to yell something back or take off running or both. Then I remember: nobody here knows me. At the far end of the store, two kids on skateboards are twisting in and out of the pathway of some scrawny blond kid about my age. He looks short next to the skateboarders, and I'm guessing he'd be shorter than they are even if they were all on the ground.

My feet freeze on the sidewalk. There's no way I'm going to dive in and help this kid, but I wish he would do something. If he swung his arm at just the right minute, he could knock one of those creeps off his feet.

"Shut up, Dembinski!" the short kid shouts. He just walks past them and, eventually, past me.

"What are *you* looking at?" the other skateboarder shouts at me as the kid on foot enters the store.

Before I can answer, a man comes up behind me. "Out of here, gentlemen! You know the rules." He raps the back of his hand on a sign attached to the store wall. "'No skateboarding on store property.' If you forget again, I'll have to call your parents."

"Yeah, yeah," the kids say, but they start skateboarding across the parking lot and, I'm relieved to see, head down the street in the opposite direction from the way I have to walk.

I start up the street toward my grandfather's house. Just how weird is it that I, Brad Stanislawski, am walking *toward* a funeral home of my own free will and that I know I'll feel safer when I get there?

7

The Baseball Game

My grandfather and I are finishing our Deluxe Frozen Entrees when the phone rings. I've already noticed that happens a lot here. You'd think he was in real estate. The last few times, he just ignored it and said "Mike will get that downstairs," but this time he gets up. "That's my private line."

"Hello?" There's a pause and then, "Rita, how are you?" In less time than it could have taken her to answer his question, he answers, "Sure, I'll put him on," and hands the phone to me.

"Hi, honey," Mom says. "I miss you already. How was your trip?"

My grandfather walks out of the room, but I keep my voice low. "Fine," I tell her. "But there's this little detail about your dad living in a funeral home that you forgot to tell me. *And* there's a dead person here."

"I should have told you. I thought there was no use raising your stress level any higher. Remember, though, I grew up there. I knew you wouldn't need to have contact with the business part."

"Gee, Mom, that makes me feel tons better." I practice the sarcasm I've gotten so good at lately. "If I see any dead people upstairs I'll just send them back downstairs where they belong."

"Very funny. I really am sorry to hear that he's got business. He can be pretty tied up when there's someone downstairs."

"Actually, it doesn't seem like a big deal so far. Mike is taking care of things for him tonight while we go to a baseball game."

"That's great." Mom sounds really surprised. "He has some help now, does he?"

"Yeah. Mike picked up the dead man while your dad was at the airport getting me."

"My dad?" she says. "You can call him Grandpa, you know."

"Right. We'll see. So, tell me about California."

"Oh, honey, I think it's going to be fun. If you're doing okay, that makes it even better for me."

My grandfather has already cleared away our plates and wiped off the table. "I'll be fine," I say, "but I guess I'd better go. We don't want the Pirates to start without us."

"All right, sweetie. You take care. I'll call again later in the week."

"Good-bye," I say, and hang up the phone.

My grandfather looks as if he's confused. "Who said anything about the Pirates?"

"You did, didn't you? You said we could go to the baseball game tonight. And the Pirates are your team, right?"

"I like the Pirates, and we can stay home and watch them on TV if that's what you'd rather do. The game I was planning to take you to is the recreation league game up at the park. I sponsor one of the teams."

"Right," I say and nod. So now I'll have two exciting items on my vacation highlights list: grocery store and non-Pirate baseball game. This place is a thrill a minute.

The park is a mile or so from my grandfather's house in the opposite direction from the store. As we drive, he points out some landmarks. There's a sign in front of his church advertising the festival that they're having in a few days. The hospital is right across the street from there. A few more houses follow, then we're at the ball-field.

Some metal bleachers sit on one side. As we start toward them, it seems like everyone we pass knows my grandfather. "How's it going, Stanley?" one guy calls. "Who's the boy?" When my grandfather tells him, he says, "Come on, he's too good-looking to be related to you." Both of them laugh.

"Hey, Stush." Another man slaps my grandfather on the back. "What's new?"

We miss almost an entire inning until we finally sit down. The team at bat has DELVECCHIO HARDWARE printed on their shirts. Sure enough, the red team in the field says STANISLAWSKI FUNERAL HOME. I'm amazed all that writing fits on the back of a shirt.

"Why did that man call you Stush?" I ask.

"It's just a nickname, a nickname for Stanley."

"Oh." I feel dumb.

"Do you have a nickname?" he asks. "What do your friends call you?"

I feel my face turn red. I bite my lip on the inside to keep it from shaking. What am I going to tell him? *They call me Stan-is-lousy to make fun of the name I got from you. And by the way, I plan to change it as soon as I'm eighteen.* I finally answer, "The kids I like just call me Brad."

My grandfather looks like he's planning to say something, but then he turns to watch the game.

The players are high school kids. Most of them are tall and skinny, but one on our team already has the kind of round belly that you usually see only on older men. After he hits a grounder past the second baseman, his whole body bounces as he runs for the base. He makes it by a split second, and all of us Stanislawski fans cheer.

"Can I get you a Coke?" my grandfather asks.

"Sure. Thanks."

I watch him as he gets off the bleachers. He's moving slowly and stiff-legged, like his knees are stuck in a sitting position. It takes him a while to reach the bottom even though we're only in the fourth row.

"Are you related to that guy?" a red-haired boy sitting a few feet to my left suddenly says.

"Are you talking to me?" I ask.

"Who else?" the kid answers in a smart-aleck sort of way.

"He's my grandfather." I hope the conversation stops there.

"You staying at his place?"

"Yeah. So what?" I stare straight ahead at the game, wishing he'll leave me alone. I clap for the next play, trying to distract him, then realize it was a Delvecchio Hardware run.

"I just thought you might want to know something for your own safety, kid," the boy mumbles, sliding closer to me on the bench.

I try not to look in his direction, but I'm just too curious.

"What do you mean, for my safety?"

"You know how dead people lay down in the caskets?"

"Yeah. So?" This kid is getting on my nerves.

"Well," he continues, "you can only see the front of their heads when they're in there. And it's a good thing, because everyone knows old man Stanislawski scalps the backs."

"Yeah, right," I say. "How would you know?"

"He keeps the scalps in a bag in his drain-the-blood room." Then, with a voice that tells me he means it, he adds, "My brother has seen it," then scoots back to where he was before.

"Here's your Coke." My grandfather sits down beside me. I jump and barely miss knocking it out of his hand.

8

The Bag of Scalps

For the rest of the game, I try to act as if nothing has
happened, but it isn't easy. I can see the redheaded kid
watching me out of the corner of my eye. When I do
glance over at him, he just nods slowly.

Who is this kid and why should I believe him? I keep
asking myself. But then another thought rushes in: *I
don't know my grandfather either.* I *do* know that my
mother didn't like him much. What if she was afraid of
him? Maybe she knows about the scalp thing and just
didn't want to tell me.

My grandfather talks about the good plays and the players he knows as if everything is normal. "You see number
seventeen, Brad? The shortstop? He's my friend Ed's son.
He's the best baseball player to come out of Wallace Corners in a long time. You can bet that boy will get a scholar-
ship somewhere if the pros don't snatch him up first."

I let him ramble on, but tune him out. Instead of listening, I watch his hands, with their thick fingers and bulging knuckles. I wonder if these are the hands of a scalper. Finally he notices that he's the only one talking. "Hey, I'm sorry. After traveling and all, you must be tired. Why don't we head home and get you to bed? It looks like we're going to win anyway."

"Sure" is all that will squeak out, but at least it gets us moving. I look at the kid on the bench again, and he gives me one last nod.

When we get back to the funeral home, my grandfather makes sure there are clean towels for me in the bathroom, then says he has some phone calls to make.

I'm so grubby from the airplane ride and the ballpark that I have to take a shower, but I set a new record for speed. Being behind the shower curtain seems scarier than just being in the house with a potential maniac. I step in before the water has even gotten warm enough, and I know there's still soap in my hair when I get out.

I'm wide awake by the time I finish taking a cold shower. That's good because between the dead bodies, open caskets, and now scalps, I've had about enough of this place. I've got a return ticket, but of course it's for the end of next week. I wonder if the airlines would take me now.

I wish I hadn't fallen asleep on the ride from the airport. I have no idea how to find my way there. If I hitch-hike, whoever picks me up ought to know the way, I guess. Mom will have a fit when she finds out, but she'll understand when I tell her about the scalps. *If* I have proof.

I know this last thought is true, and it may be the scariest thing of all: I need to find the bag of scalps before I go. I can't just tell Mom, "I ran away because I heard a creepy rumor." I need to see the evidence with my own eyes.

I dress for bed and turn out the light. I hear my grand-father come to the doorway a few minutes later. He doesn't say anything, so he must think I'm asleep.

He pulls the door most of the way closed behind him, so I can't tell if he's getting ready for bed yet or not. I try hard to listen for noise, but the next thing I know, I'm waking up from a nightmare: My grandfather is standing in front of me, holding a knife in one hand and a dripping, bloody scalp in the other!

I spring up in bed. My heart's pounding, and my T-shirt is damp. The room is dark, but the curtains are open, and there's light coming in from the streetlamp. If I'm going to find those scalps, this is the time to do it. I take slow, deep breaths until my chest stops pounding, then I make myself get out of bed.

The door isn't shut all the way, so it doesn't make

noise when I push past it. There's a night-light glowing from the bathroom. The rest of the hall is dark. I tiptoe past my grandfather's room and toward the living room.

I wonder if there's another way down to the basement, like a back set of stairs, but it's too late to try and find my way around now. I shuffle my feet in tiny steps, hoping that if I kick something it won't make me trip. I haven't noticed where the cat's bed is. If I tramp on her, I could be a goner.

Feeling my way, I make it to the front door of the second floor. Of course, it's closed tightly. I don't think my grandfather set any kind of alarm system. Still, it takes a long time to ease the door open silently. When I finally make my way through the doorway, there's a handrail and the steps are carpeted so I can move a little faster.

At the bottom of the stairs, I need to open the door into the funeral home, but I stop. I know Mr. Chihoski is in there in his casket. His family is coming to look at him tomorrow.

My mouth is getting dry, but I have to keep going. I want to see those scalps for myself, and then I've got to get out of here.

I open the door to the funeral home. A little bit of street light comes in to my right through the front door window. It's not bright enough for me to see the casket, but it shines enough light on the hallway that I can find my way. I set one foot on the carpet, then rush the length of it. I feel like the ghost of Mr. Chihoski can't hurt me if I get past him quickly.

It's darker at the end of the hall. I feel along the wall and push a big door open to another set of stairs. I find a handrail and follow the stairs down.

When I'm at the bottom, I feel around for a door, but find a light switch instead. I'm two floors below my grandfather now, so the light shouldn't be a problem. I switch it on, and a bulb lights up overhead.

There are closed doors to my left and right. I gently turn the handle on the left door first and pull it open. I can barely make out the side of my grandfather's car. This is just the garage. I close that door.

I realize that the door on the right must be the one I'm looking for. I slowly try the knob, and it opens, too. As I put my hand around the corner of the room to find another light switch, a strong odor hits me. It's the same nasty smell we had in our classroom the day the science teacher demonstrated a frog dissection.

When I flick the switch, the lights hum quietly, then they burst on at once. The ceiling has lots of fluorescent bulbs, and suddenly it's as bright as the grocery store.

I walk in just a few steps. A large white table sits in the middle of the room. It looks like something you might find in a hospital or Frankenstein's laboratory. Luckily, there's nothing—that is, *no one*—on it. A big stainless-steel sink is attached to the wall, and several pieces of plastic tubing are draped from a rack above it. A shirt like the one Mike was wearing hangs from a hook on the wall, and a white doctor's coat sticks out underneath it.

I don't see much else except for some shelves and cabinets and a small window near the ceiling. I take another step inside. When I do, I spot a large grocery bag sitting on the floor by the wall. The shape of the bag tells me that it's full, and all I can see coming out the top is a patch of brown hair.

My heart starts to pound, but I walk toward the bag anyway. The kid was right. My grandfather really scalps people. Suddenly, I hear footsteps behind me. I spin toward the door.

"Bradley! What on earth are you doing down here?"

9

My Grandfather Explains the Scalp Bag

My grandfather is blocking the door. There's no way I can dart past him. I'm caught anyway, so I just blurt out the truth. Pointing to the scalp bag, I stammer, "A kid at the baseball game told me about the scalps. I just wanted to see for myself." I start to shiver all over. To make my arms stop, I cross them in front of me. "I'd like to leave now, please." I try to sound tough, but the tingle in my nose says there's a chance I might cry.

He walks into the room and looks where I'm pointing. He shakes his head as he approaches the bag, then glances up at the small window near the ceiling. "I'm going to have to pin the curtain shut," he says. "I've heard kids messing around before. This time they've gone too far, scaring you like that."

He carries the bag to the big table, tips it over, and spills out some of the stuff inside. Under the lights, I can see that it isn't all hair. Some of it looks like fur and feathers, too. He holds up the hairy piece that I saw on top. "Muskrat pelt," he says. He lifts several more of the pieces one by one. "Beaver. Rabbit. Moose. Chicken neck. Quail feathers. Turkey. Peacock."

"You're a hunter?" I ask, finding that I can breathe again.

"No," he says, "I'm a fisherman. These are fly-tying materials."

I've heard of fly fishing. I guess that's what he's talking about. I know it's none of my business, but I still yell, "Well, what are they doing in the drain-the-blood room?"

My grandfather smiles for a second. "That's what they call it?" Then he says, "It's cooler down here. This material is expensive, and I want it to last."

He starts lifting everything back into the bag. When it's full again, he picks it up and carries it toward the door. He puts his hand on my shoulder and leads me out of the room. I stop myself from shaking it off.

"After we've both had a good night's sleep," he says, "I can show you a little something about the art of tying flies. How would that be?"

I yawn before I can answer. I feel like I haven't slept in a month. "I guess," I say. "Sure."

It's after ten in the morning by the time I get up and dress. I head to the kitchen to find some breakfast. My grandfather isn't around, but there's a note on the table.

Help yourself, Brad. I have some errands to run. See
you around lunchtime. No need to lock the door if you
go out. Mike is downstairs.

                                            —Grandpa

He has laid out dishes and silverware, and there's
cereal, bread, and peanut butter on the table. I make
myself a peanut butter sandwich and wash it down with a
glass of milk. It's exactly what I would have had at home.
Maybe all these years I've been eating "bachelor food"
and didn't even know it.

I decide to walk to the baseball park, since the only
other place I know to go is the store, and I can't think
of anything I need. I take my sketchbook and pencil
with me.

On the way out, I pass the door into the funeral home.
It's open, and Mike is in there, moving baskets of flowers
from one stand to another. Mr. Chihoski is in the casket,
but with Mike walking around and all the lights on, he
doesn't look very scary. I stop in the doorway.

Whispering, I say, "Hi, Mike."

"Oh, hi," he answers in a normal, loud voice. I must
look surprised because he says, "It's okay. We can talk.
The family won't be in for a couple of hours yet. What
have you got there?" he asks. Mike puts a small basket
of flowers on a stand near old Walter's head.

I hand Mike my book. It feels funny, since I just met

him. My art teacher and English teacher are about the only ones who ever see my drawings. And Mom. The art teacher at my last school told me what an interesting style I had and how he was really more experienced in teaching realistic art, but he admired my fantasy drawings, as he called them. The English teacher never commented. She just took my book when I got caught drawing in class. She always looked to see what I'd been working on, and I saw her smile twice.

"This is some really cool stuff," Mike says, turning the pages. "I guess you come by your talent honestly. Your grandpa is a bit of an artist, too."

"He is?" I ask.

"Sure. Has he shown you the flies he makes for fishing?"

"No. He told me about them last night, though. He said he'll show me how today."

"You'll enjoy that. He's got a real flair for it."

"Does he do any other art stuff?" I ask.

"He makes his living with it." He points to Mr. Chihoski. "Making the deceased look good takes an artist's touch. I've finished my funeral director's schooling, but I know it will be years until I'll be as good as your grandpa. It's one of the things I'm trying to learn while I'm here."

"You don't plan to stay?"

"Well, that's up to him. Now that my apprenticeship is

over—my training time—I'm ready to look for a partnership. I'm not sure he wants that. He's used to doing things his own way."

I remember how my grandfather seemed mad at Mike yesterday. Chances are he's not too easy to work for.

Mike hands my sketchbook back and grabs another flower basket.

"See you later," I say, and head out into the street.

It only takes about fifteen minutes to walk to the ballfield. There's no game going on, so I climb up on the bleachers and open my sketchbook. I look around for something to draw and see a huge tree at the edge of the field. It's old and twisty with big leaves that whoosh in the wind. It would be great for a tree house. In my picture, I twirl one of the limbs so that it looks like an arm. On the hand part of the arm, I add a gnome. Strange faces are my favorite thing to draw, and this one comes easy. His hair sticks straight up in the air, just like that kid's on the skateboard outside the store yesterday. His ears are too wide, and, since he's a gnome, they're pointy. I write "World's Weirdest Gnome" under the picture. Then I remember hearing the kid's name: Dembinski. I change the title to read "Dumbski, the World's Weirdest Gnome."

I look at the picture again. How does a guy with a name like Dembinski get away with picking on other kids? That name's even worse than Stanislawski. What would Anthony and Jason do with it? "Hey, Dumbo!" they'd say. Since his ears stick out, too, they'd probably call him Dumbo the Flying Elephant, or something dopey like that.

I try to picture Dembinski getting picked on. I look at my drawing to see if I can make him look scared, but it doesn't seem to fit. I don't even know the kid, and somehow I'd bet Anthony and Jason wouldn't get to him at all.

I rip the picture in half and pitch it in the trash barrel.

As I walk out toward the street, a couple of kids race into the park on their bikes. Immediately, my brain flies back to the trash barrel. Did those kids get a good look at me, or, worse yet, did I sign the picture before I pitched it? I can't remember. Just in case, I don't waste any time getting home.

10

The Art of Tying Flies

I have lunch with my grandfather. As soon as we clean up the table, he keeps his promise and brings out the bag of fly-tying stuff and a box full of other supplies. "Pull up a chair beside me," he says, and I do.

He starts by clamping a tool to the edge of the table. "This is the vise. It will hold everything still while we're making it and keep us from getting our fingers hooked." He looks through several boxes of hooks and picks out a small one. "We'll start with a number fourteen," he says, attaching it to the end of the vise.

"I thought fishermen just put worms on their hooks," I say.

"That's bait fishing. Fly fishing is different. It's all about trying to outsmart the fish. Part of that comes in the fishing, and part of it is in the fly. If I do everything right, the fish thinks he's about to eat a real insect." He points to a spool on the table. "I'll start with that wire, please. It's made of lead."

I hand it to him. "So the fish only like to eat flies? Why do you bother with all this other stuff?"

"What we call a fly is an imitation insect attached to a hook. Any insect. There are lots of different kinds because you never know what the fish will be hungry for. He might have been snacking on mosquitoes all week—"

"And now he's hungry for a dragonfly?" I say.

"Exactly," he agrees. His hands are starting to twirl things around the hook.

"So what kind are you making?" I ask.

"This one is called a Hare's Ear." He adjusts his glasses and then continues. "It's a nymph, a baby insect, so I'll drag it under the water to fish with it. That's why I need the lead first. I don't want it to float."

"So how do you make it look real? That rabbit fur doesn't look like an insect to me."

"Did you ever study insects in school?" he asks. "Remember their parts?"

I think for a while. "They have a head and an abdomen," I say finally. "And something else. A thorax?"

"Hey, they're teaching you something important in school," he says, laughing. "Those parts are all you really have to remember to tie a good fly. Hand me the pheasant, will you?"

I feel like I'm assisting a doctor during an operation. But instead of scalpel and clamps, he asks for different stuff: gold thread, hare (which somehow makes it sound less sad than saying "bunny"), turkey quill, rooster feather. Each piece adds a new layer, but the whole fly is less than an inch long.

He keeps talking as he puts it together. "I'm going to fuzz a little bit of the rabbit fur with my fingers to make the abdomen. See how I create the body segments by wrapping the thread? The turkey quill makes the thorax. The chicken feathers create the legs. Add some more fur. Trim it just so."

Sure enough, instead of looking like a hook with a bunch of animal pieces attached to it, it looks like a real insect in three segments. And it took him only a couple of minutes to make it.

"Ready to try it?" he asks.

"Me? I don't even fish."

"Go ahead. I'm guessing you've got that great Stanislawski touch."

"Okay." I change seats with him. "I don't know how good it will be."

It's even harder than it looked. I feel dumb every time I do something wrong, and I'm ready to quit if my grandfather yells at me. He doesn't yell, though. He just corrects my moves, telling me to tighten the thread or loosen it, and we keep going. It takes me forty-five minutes and a lot of frustration, but I eventually finish a fatter version of the fly my grandfather made. "Ta-da!" I say. It's not perfect, but I feel proud anyway.

"You're destined to be a great fisherman. Would you like to try and catch something with this?"

"I guess. When?"

"Tomorrow is probably fine. It's Mike's day off, but I should be free after the funeral." He gets up from his chair. "You go ahead and make some more if you like. Make the same one or try something else." He hands me a thick book called *Fly-Tying Techniques*. "I'm sure the fish will be happy to see something new on the menu."

I spend the afternoon making two more Hare's Ears. I start working again after supper. Two mayflies and a caddis later, it's time for bed.

My grandfather comes into my room as I'm lining the flies up on the desk. He's got a beige vest in his hands.

"I'm sorry I don't have anything new," he says. "But I've got an extra fishing vest for you to use, if you'd like."

"Thanks." I try it on. "Hey, it fits."

"Actually, that one belonged to your mother many years ago."

"Mom used to fish? She never told me that."

"I don't suppose she's told you very much about her growing-up years."

When I don't answer, he keeps talking. "You'll have to ask her about the day she landed more fish than I did. I'll bet she still remembers that one." He hangs the vest over the back of the desk chair. "You get some sleep now. Dream of catching the big one."

I go to bed and think about all the things I didn't know a day ago. It makes me wonder what else my grandfather's going to spring on me.

11

The Phone in the Night

It's the middle of the night, and I've just finished using the bathroom when the phone rings. I hear my grandfather in his bedroom clearing his throat a couple of times before he picks it up. "Stanislawski Funeral Home," he says. I guess it must be his business line. I see a light go on in his room.

"Yes. Okay," he says. "And what's the first name?"

I walk toward his room to see what's happening.

"All right. I'll be right there." He hangs up the phone.

I knock on the frame of his open door and say, "What's up?" I don't know what time it is, but I feel wide awake.

He's buckling the belt on his pants and reaching for a shirt on the chair. "I've got to pick up a body at the hospital. It never fails. Every time Mike plans to be out of town on his day off, we get a call during the night, and I'm left to do everything myself."

I have no idea what I'm volunteering for, but I blurt out, "I could help."

He stops buttoning for a minute and looks at me. He seems to be sizing me up. For once my size might come in handy. "Well, you look pretty strong for a kid. If you'd like to help, hurry and get dressed."

I head back to my room and turn on the light. "Pants, not shorts," he yells after me. "And wear your sneakers, not your sandals."

It only takes a minute to get my jeans, shirt, shoes, and socks on. I whip a comb through my hair, then head out of the room.

"Should I brush my teeth or anything?" I ask.

"You don't have to bother. You won't be talking to anyone," he says.

I guess that's a nice way of saying, "Keep quiet while we're there."

We go down into the garage. My grandfather pushes the automatic door-opener, and the lights go on. There's a full-sized station wagon parked next to his fancy car. He opens the back of it.

"Give me a hand with this," he says. He sounds bossy, but I don't mind. Now that I've volunteered, I want to see where we're going. I help him pull out a big metal tray that looks like a giant cookie sheet. We lean it against the wall at the end of the garage. "This is what my help uses to hold the flowers when they transfer them to the cemetery. It was ready for tomorrow." He looks at his watch and corrects himself. "I mean today.

"We need to put the gurney in." He walks into the drain-the-blood room and rolls out a portable bed on wheels. I didn't see it there yesterday, so maybe he usually keeps it in the back of the station wagon. There's some sort of canvas sleeping bag on top of it.

My grandfather steers it to the rear station wagon door. "Stand on the other side and help me put this in," he says. He rolls the bed up to the back, and as we push it in, the legs fold underneath it. It all looks a lot like ambulance shows on TV, but not as fancy. Except for being roomier than most station wagons, this one doesn't seem to be anything unusual.

There are about a thousand questions I'd like to ask as we drive to the hospital, but my grandfather's very quiet. It seems like he's forgotten I'm here, so I just keep my mouth shut and ride.

When we get to the hospital, we park near a back entrance. I follow my grandfather around the station wagon. "Help me with the gurney, Brad," he says.

I open my mouth and almost answer, "We have to go in there to get it?" But I swallow without letting the words come out. I guess I haven't given this whole operation much thought. Did I expect the person to be waiting for us in the parking lot?

"She's still in the intensive care area," he says.

"It's a lady?" I ask.

"Yes. Mrs. Mihalko from down on Seventh Street," as if I should know who or where that is. "Your grandmother knew her."

That's the end of our conversation again until we wheel up in front of the glass door with INTENSIVE CARE printed on it.

I hold the door for him, and he guides the bed in. A nurse who has been checking on some other patient walks over to meet us. When she sees me, she turns back to the other beds and pulls a curtain around each of them. She must think that the living patients would scare me more than the dead one, and from what I saw, she's probably right. Afterward she says, "Over here, Mr. Stanislawski."

We follow her to the last bed. There's a curtain around it, too, and she pulls it back. An old lady is lying there. I don't see any difference between her and the other patients except that they've got tubes hooking them up to noisy machines and she doesn't. She looks like she's just sleeping.

The nurse and my grandfather both know what to do. The dead lady needs to be moved off her bed and onto ours. He unzips the canvas bag the whole way to the bottom. When he says "Help us to lift, Brad," I'm relieved to find that I'm only touching sheets, not arms or legs. I'm sure this was a nice lady, but the whole thing still gives me the creeps. I try to lift without looking.

My grandfather zips the bag closed and signs a paper on the clipboard that the nurse gives him. He thanks her, and we're off again.

Getting the gurney into the back of the station wagon is harder now than when it was empty. Once we do, it takes only a few minutes to drive back home. It's a cool night, but as we move the gurney out and into the embalming room, I can see there's sweat on my grandfather's forehead.

"Thanks for the help. You can go back up to bed now," he says after we're finished. "I have some work to do here."

"I could help you." But as my mouth makes the offer, my brain is screaming, "Please don't make me!"

"Thanks anyway," he says. "Go on now."

I start toward the stairs.

"Oh, Brad," he adds, "I guess you know we're going to have to put off fishing for a day or so."

My mother was right: When he's busy at the funeral home, my grandfather isn't much fun. But I, Brad Stanislawski, Actor of the Year, let him off the hook. I tell him, "No problem. Good night."

12

Mom's News

I'm in no hurry to get up, since I was playing funeral assistant half the night. When I finally drag myself out of bed, I hear car doors closing. I look out the window, and there's a hearse and a whole line of cars behind it. Old Walter's funeral must be moving out just in time to let Mrs. Mihalko move in.

I have some breakfast and flip through the newspaper that my grandfather left on the table. It's only about as thick as one section of the *Denver Post,* but it carries the same comics, which is all I usually look at anyway. When I'm older, people are going to be reading my comic strip in the newspaper, even in Wallace Corners, Pennsylvania.

My grandfather isn't going to be around much today, and I don't know where he put the fly-tying stuff, so I decide to kill some time in town. I get dressed, grab my wallet, and write him a note.

I've gone out looking for trouble. Ha ha. See you later.

—Brad

I'm heading for the door when the phone rings. I can see by the light on the phone that it's the private line, so I pick it up and say hello.

"Bradley?" It's Mom.

"Hi, Mom. How are you?"

"Honey, I am just unbelievably fine," she says.

"That's good. Tell me about California."

"I'm having a great time. You will never in a million years guess what I did yesterday."

I think back to what she had on her California wish list. "You were in the audience at a game show."

"I got to be *on* a game show!" she says. "They taped it, so we'll be able to see me on TV next month. Can you believe it?"

"That's great. So did you win us a new car? Or are we on our way to Jamaica?"

"Actually, I didn't do too well in the prize department. But I did meet a nice man who was another contestant. His name's David. We're going out to dinner tonight."

"Personally, Mom, I would rather have had the car."

"Very funny. How about you? Are you doing anything interesting?"

I have a feeling that going to the hospital in the middle of the night isn't what she has in mind, so I figure

I'll save that story for when I get home. "Well, yesterday your dad showed me how to tie flies, and I made some myself."

"You're brave. I only lasted for about ten minutes of fly-tying lessons before he growled at me and I quit. Don't let him push you to do that stuff if you don't want to."

Something in my mom's voice makes me feel sorry for her, and for my grandfather, too. "It's fine," I say. "He didn't growl."

"So, is anything else happening?"

"Not really. We might go fishing later. Hey, that reminds me, he said you used to fish. You never told me that."

Mom sounds annoyed when she answers me. "That was a long time ago, and I was never very good at it." She pauses for a second, then sounds a little happier when she says, "I do remember one day when I caught more fish than Dad did, though. I enjoyed that."

"He remembers it, too," I tell her. "I'm going to use your old vest when we go."

"He still has my vest?" She sounds a lot quieter now. "I would have thought that got thrown away years ago."

"It's still here. You don't mind, do you?"

She pauses for a second. "No," she says. "Of course not."

"He's tied up with the funeral business today, so I'm going to check out some more of the town."

She starts to laugh. "That won't take long, but I'll let

you go now. I want a full report on whether the old burg has changed any since I was hanging around there."

I put on a voice like a TV newsman. "Preliminary findings suggest the town of Wallace Corners is frozen in time. Details at eleven."

"All right, crazy boy. You take care. I miss you."

"I miss you, too, Mom. Good-bye."

I hang up and head out the door. I start walking in the direction of the store, since that's as far as I got last time. It's warming up fast, and the sun is really bright. Good thing the trees make the sidewalk shady.

I cruise past all the little businesses I saw the other day. I don't know how far this town reaches, but it can't be too far. Mom told me there were only about six thousand people here when she was growing up, and it probably hasn't grown any. Once I pass the store, I see more of the business district. There's a post office, a couple of bars, and another little church. I have to remember to ask my grandfather about all the churches. This must be the most religious place on the face of the earth.

There's a large school building at the end of the street. After that the houses seem to be more spread out, so I guess I've about reached the end of the line in Wallace Corners. I decide to walk around the school before heading back.

I go toward the left of the building. The gym sticks

out at that end. It doesn't match the rest of the building, since it's newer and pretty big. Probably athletes are king here, just like at home.

The school looks locked up tight for the summer, but there's an outdoor basketball court behind the gym, and I can hear somebody shooting baskets. I skirt around the edge of the court, not paying attention to who's there. Basketball isn't my game anyway.

I'm around the court and almost to the school wall when I hear the shooter yelling, "Hey, Stanislawski, is that you?"

I stop and turn around slowly. I'm relieved to see it's only the redhaired kid from the baseball game. He jogs over to me.

"Well, I see you still have all your hair. He didn't scalp you yet. Congratulations," he says, grinning.

"It's a wig," I tell him, tapping myself on the head. "Looks okay, though, don't you think?"

He starts to laugh. Finally, a kid who gets my sense of humor.

"My name's Pat Robinson. If you hear someone talk about Freckles, that's me, but I like Pat better."

It would have been a miracle if Pat could have gone through life *without* someone calling him Freckles. His face, arms, and legs look like someone splatter-painted him with brown stain.

I put my hand out to shake. "Hi, Pat. My name's Brad."

"So, did you check out the scalp collection?"

"Yeah. It's not what it looks like. I investigated personally."

"You went in the drain-the-blood room? I'm impressed." I can tell from Pat's voice that he means it.

"Hey, it wasn't so scary," though saying the words makes a chill spin up my arms and neck. I hope it doesn't show.

"So, have you tried lying in any caskets?" he asks. "If I were you, that's what I'd be doing right now."

"I can sleep in one if I want to," I say, trying to sound casual, "but the bed's more comfortable."

Pat raises his eyebrows. "Oh, yeah?"

He holds his hand over his eyes to block the sun as he squints up at me. "You know, I could use some help with this thing I've been working on. Feel like giving me a hand?"

I have nothing better to do. Besides, it's nice to have somebody wanting me around. Without bothering to ask what "this thing" is, I answer, "Sure."

13

The House

Pat bounce-passes his basketball to me, picks up his bike from the grass at the edge of the court, and rides over to where I'm standing. He moves forward, off the seat. "Come on," he says. "You hold the ball, and I'll be the taxi."

We don't say much for the first couple of blocks, but when we start going uphill on a side street I haven't seen before, Pat starts whining.

"This was a bad idea," he moans. "You weigh a ton."

I just laugh, but I also notice that we're slowing down. Maybe he really can't tow me.

"You want me to get off?" I ask, feeling weird for outsizing yet another kid my age.

"No," he says, stopping the bike, "I want you to take your turn."

"And my turn just happens to be up the hill?"

"You got it." He gets off and reaches for the ball so that we can trade places.

I move forward and start pedaling. The first couple of churns are tough, but once we get going it's not too bad.

We've gone up the hill for two blocks and turned left for another two when Pat tells me to pull over. We're in a neighborhood that looks different from the rest of the town, like rich people lived here once. The houses are larger and farther apart than the ones near the funeral home, but they don't seem any newer. In fact, they might be older. The tall stone-block walls probably look the same as they did the day they were built; everything else could use a coat of paint.

We get off the bike, and Pat jogs it to the back wall that surrounds the house. He stashes the bike behind a bush. I guess his mom is as picky as mine about putting things away. He's likely hiding it so he won't have to haul it to the garage or something.

He waves for me to follow him through an old iron gate and uphill into the long backyard full of high grass and big trees. I'm already sweaty from the ride up the hill, and it's not any cooler as I jog to keep up.

"Boy, you've got a big house," I call as I catch up. "Are there a lot of kids in your family?"

Pat turns to me long enough to say, "Zip it, would you?" then keeps hurrying.

We're both panting a little when we reach the house. Pat's all hand signals again as he opens a wooden gate into a small side yard. He closes it behind us and plops down in the grass. I just stand there looking at him until he says, "Sit down."

I'd rather not get chewed out again for breathing, so I whisper, "What's going on?"

He starts laughing as if I just said something hilarious. About two more seconds of this and I'm out of here.

He finally settles down and says, "This isn't my house, dope. It's just a place where I'm trying to do a little research."

"Research?"

"Yeah. There hasn't been anybody living in this old place for years, but I guess the owners are fixing it up to sell or something. I've seen guys working here off and on for weeks."

"So?" I ask. I don't think he's said anything that made sense since we left the school.

"So the workers left a ladder here." He pauses as if that explains everything. When I don't say anything, he says, "Don't you get it? We can get in and check this place out."

I still feel like he's speaking Greek. "Why would we want to get in?" I ask.

"For the fun of it, goofball." He shakes his head and

71

stays quiet for a minute. When he starts to talk again, it's as if we're friends and I'm not the dimmest bulb in the closet. "Look, Brad, I don't want to break anything. I just want to look around. Like Huck Finn and Tom Sawyer. Finding some adventure in this town isn't that easy, in case you haven't noticed. You've got to take it where you can."

"What makes you think we won't get in trouble?" I ask.

"They probably expect people to drop in. The ladder's against the house, for crying out loud. It's like an invitation." He points down the side of the house where, sure enough, there is a ladder leaning.

He pats my shoulder a couple of times, then says, "Come on, buddy, let's check it out."

We walk along the house to the base of the ladder. It's one of those supersize industrial ones with ropes attached. There's no way Pat and I are going to be able to move it, and there's no window anywhere near it.

"Well, I guess that plan didn't last long," I tell him. "We can't move this thing, and there aren't any windows close to it."

He points over our heads, and the sun coming through the trees blasts into my face. "What's the matter with that window?" he asks.

11

The Climb

"You've got to be kidding!" I yell, forgetting to be quiet. But the truth is, I don't think anyone could see or hear us anyway. The part of the house that the ladder is leaning on is hidden from the street by the wall and a lot of tall, leafy trees. There's a good breeze going, too, so the trees are covering us with their rustling.

"Why would I be kidding?" Pat asks. "You know how these ladders work, don't you?" He doesn't wait for me to answer. "You just pull a couple of these ropes and it gets twice as high. And see?" He points again at the window just to the left of the clouds. "They even left it open for us. What do you say?"

I don't say anything. I just stand there wiping my sweaty palms on my pants. That must be enough of a yes for Pat, because he takes one of the ropes and starts giving orders. "Grab this one as high as you can reach. That's right. Pull it on three. One. Two . . ."

At three, I find myself throwing my weight onto the rope, and Pat and I are playing tug-of-war against the ladder. More directions, more one-two-threes, and the ladder crawls up the side. When we're finished, it leans high against the house, just a few feet short of the windowsill.

"Man, you've got some muscles," Pat says. "That was easier than I thought it would be."

The compliment makes me smile.

"So," he says, "do you want to go up first, or should I?"

My smile fades fast. "You go first. I'll hold the ladder steady."

I'm hoping that he'll find mountains of treasure up there, get distracted, and forget I'm even here. A trip from earth to sky by way of this ladder does not sound like my idea of a good time.

Pat starts moving—hand, foot, hand, foot—as if he's been scaling ladders all his life. If he's scared, he's not showing it. I watch him climb for a while, but after the halfway point a puffy cloud starts moving across the sky above him. My feet are planted on the ground, but I get dizzy just looking at it. I stare at the grass instead and hold the ladder with my arms stretched in front of me.

I've been leaning like that for a couple of minutes when I feel the ladder start to shake. I look up in time to duck away from Pat's foot. Another step and it would have come down on my head.

"No treasures up there?" I ask, feeling much better now that I know this will all be over soon.

"Weren't you even watching, Stanislawski? I got the whole way up there, but my reach was a foot short. You and your long arms are going to have to go first. When you get inside, you can come downstairs and let me in."

I open my mouth to say something, but nothing comes out. Finally, I squeak, "I don't know."

"Aw, come on. You're not going to let me down after all this, are you?" His shoulders slump like I just punched him in the stomach.

Let him down or climb up—I wish I didn't have to do either. I guess I must not want to let him down even more than I don't want to climb up because eventually I say, "I'll try."

I wipe my hands on my thighs, grab the first rung above my head, step onto the bottom rung, and push off. Climbing like Pat did—hand, foot, hand, foot—I feel like I'm dangling in air. I'm afraid Pat will laugh, but I switch to hand, hand, foot, foot, like a little kid who's just learning to go up the steps.

I focus on the wall behind each rung. Paint is peeling in long, curly chunks. If I dared to let go of the ladder, it would be neat to see how much you could peel off without making it crumble.

The ladder is steep, and the higher I go, the harder I

have to pull myself. When the breeze blows, the leaves and branches brush against me. My mouth is so dry I can hardly swallow. I heave my hand up for the next rung, but grab only air. Instantly, my balance is gone. Forcing my body against the rungs, I jerk my head upward, squint at the sun and the roof above me, and focus on the windowsill. I'm at the top.

"You can reach it, right, Stanislawski?" Hearing Pat's voice from far below sends chills up my back.

Pressing against the rungs, I paw at the wall above me. The breeze throws paint flakes at me, and I turn to avoid the grit.

"You're really close! Just stretch!" My fingers obey and land on the ridge of the sill.

Pat yells, "Can you get in?"

"I'm not sure," I call back.

I don't want to lose face, so I'm going to have to at least try. Obviously, I can't do a one-armed swing onto the sill, so I bring both arms back to the ladder. Leaning my weight forward, I test my balance by moving my hands off the ladder in a gentle, flapping motion.

"You can't fly to that window," Pat bellows. "You might try climbing, though. And sometime today."

"Very funny," I call. Worrying about getting killed isn't enough; I have to try not to look stupid, either.

I reach again. My left hand finds the sill. My right

hand grabs air for a couple of seconds, then, finally, I can feel the sill with my wrist. My fingers close on a fistful of grass.

Suddenly, a huge bird dives and screeches past my head. I cover my face with my left arm, but it doesn't offer much protection. I can feel the bird grazing my back on his second pass.

I pull my right arm back to the ladder and start to climb down, but retreat isn't enough to make the bird happy. The screeches continue as he repeatedly soars around me.

I scramble down as fast as I can. I'm moving so quickly that when my foot reaches the bottom I take an extra step and land hard on the ground. I start to crab-walk backward before I realize that the bird is done with me. He's probably gone back to rebuilding the nest.

Pat puts his hand out to help me up. My legs feel like Jell-O. I don't even know if I'll be able to stand, but somehow I do. I look at Pat, and see that he's grinning at me like a crazy man.

"Stanislawski, that was the coolest thing I've ever seen!"

15

Following the Leader

It's a good thing the ride back to the funeral home is mostly downhill, because Pat takes his turn as the bike pedaler. I don't think my legs could handle it right now. We don't talk much as we ride, and the breeze feels good on my sweaty skin. My heart has finally stopped pounding and my breathing is normal again, but every block or so I get a chill up my back that reminds me what it felt like to be on the ladder.

It doesn't take long before Pat pulls up in front of the funeral home. "This is my stop," I say.

Pat gets off and wipes his forehead with the back of his arm. "Do you think I could bum a soda? A glass of water, even? It's really hot."

"Sure," I say. "Come on up. You can put your bike beside the house."

We sit and drink our Cokes in front of the open kitchen window. "Did you see the size of that bird?" Pat asks, then starts to replay our climbs in reverse. The more he talks, the more it sounds like we enjoyed ourselves and weren't just lucky to escape with our lives. By the time we finish our drinks, I feel better. When he suggests we go up to the ballpark, I agree.

As we start down the stairs, Pat points. "Is that the door to the funeral home?"

"Yeah," I say.

"Got any stiffs today?"

That line takes a minute to register. I finally answer, "There's a viewing for someone this evening, I think. She died during the night." Something stops me from telling him about the trip to the hospital. It would make a great story, but I really don't want him calling my grandmother's dead friend a stiff.

"So can we take a peek?" he asks, pointing again to the business door.

"What for?" I ask. "I thought you wanted to go to the park."

"We'll get there," he says, moving forward and opening the door.

Some of the lights are on, but I don't see either Mike or my grandfather. Luckily, dead Mrs. Mihalko isn't there either. Three baskets of funeral flowers are sitting inside the doorway. I guess the flower shop delivers them only that far.

Pat stays two steps ahead of me, and that makes me nervous.

"Mike?" I call quietly. "Hello?" No one answers.

"Well, as long as we're here, why don't you give me the grand tour?" Pat says. "Where do they keep the caskets?"

The truth is that I have no idea. When I came in the first day, they were on display, but I know they don't stay that way when there's a viewing. My grandfather must move them.

"Hey," I call, still trying to keep up with him. "Let's get out of here."

"What happened to showing me the casket you might get to sleep in?"

"Yeah, well, maybe some other time," I say, grabbing his arm. He shakes me off and uses his other hand to slide open a door I hadn't noticed before.

"Bingo!" he says, stepping inside. There are at least a dozen closed caskets in here, lined up in rows.

"We have to go, Pat," I tell him. "Come on."

He's ignoring me completely now, as if he can't hear me. He runs his hand along the top of a blue casket.

"So what do you think it's like in there?" he asks.

"When you're dead, you'll find out. Now let's go," I tell him more firmly.

His hand is still moving along the casket. "What do you think opens it? Do you think there's a remote control?"

I look down the hall, afraid that Mike or my grandfather will come—or secretly hoping they will—but the hall's still empty.

"Maybe you need a key. Hey," he says, his eyes shooting wide open. "This one's not locked!" Right away he starts struggling with the lid. "Help me with this, will you?"

I can't make him leave, but I'm sure not going to help. "No!" I tell him. "Leave it alone already." I sound like an angry grown-up, but Pat still ignores me. He leans into the lid and grunts as he strains. Finally, his arms find the right leverage. He hoists the lid, holding it just short of balancing it above his head.

A yell breaks out of both of us at once. Pat Robinson is face-to-face with dead Mrs. Mihalko, lying in the casket. A second later, the lid is on its way down.

16

Respect

I know I should try to keep the lid from crashing, but the shock makes me jump back. Before I snap out of it, my grandfather's arm shoots past me from out of nowhere, grabbing the lid just before it closes.

"What's going on here?" he yells.

Pat stands straight and wipes his hands on his jeans. His freckles look twice as brown, since his face has turned completely white. I don't know if the dropping lid, Mrs. Mihalko's dead body, or my grandfather has him more scared. He sounds as if he's trying to make a joke when he says, "Gee, that was pretty heavy."

I can tell by my grandfather's face that this is no time for jokes. "Come on. Let's go," I mumble to Pat.

"No. It's time for your friend to leave," my grandfather says as he smooths the fabric around the edge of Mrs. Mihalko's casket and closes the lid again. When he's finished, he turns to me and says, "As for you, young man, I think you'd better go to your room."

Pat takes off down the hall. "Later, Brad" is all he has a chance to say before he's gone.

"We didn't mean to hurt anything," I say quietly.

My grandfather's mouth looks tight, like he's chewing on something that tastes awful. He doesn't look at me. "I told you to go to your room."

I go upstairs and slam the bedroom door, even though I'm sure he can't hear it from downstairs. My sketchpad is on the dresser, and I grab it and start to draw. My pencil swings into making the bird that attacked me on the ladder. *No wonder my mother didn't like her father. He's nothing but mean.* I'm just starting on the flapping bird's wings when there's a knock at the door. I stash the sketchpad behind me.

My grandfather walks in, pulls the chair out from the desk, and sits. I'm not looking at his face, but I can tell he's not looking at mine either. He's staring down at his hands when he finally starts to talk. "What you did today was very foolish."

I don't say anything, but I feel my teeth clench. He's not yelling, but he might as well be.

"If that lid had dropped on that boy's neck . . . even if it had only dropped on his hands, he could have been badly hurt." He pauses a second. "That was the Robinson kid, wasn't it?"

"Yeah. So what?"

"He seems to be always looking for trouble, and he'll probably keep finding it."

"He's my friend, and he's not always looking for trouble." Climbing the ladder this afternoon pops into my head, and I can feel my face getting red.

My grandfather ignores the comment. He just stops and looks down at his hands some more, then shakes his head and starts again. "I'm ashamed of your behavior today. What you boys were up to was simply disrespectful."

He pauses like he's waiting for an answer. When I don't give him one, he keeps talking. "My whole business depends on my reputation, on my good name. 'Stanislawski' has to stand for respect."

"You've got to be kidding," I burst out, almost yelling. I know I shouldn't be talking to my grandfather this way, but I don't seem to be able to shut up. "'Stan-is-lousy' is the stupidest name! How can it stand for respect when all anyone ever does is laugh at it?"

I look directly at my grandfather now. He seems confused and upset at the same time. "What are you talking about?" he asks.

"I'm talking about being made fun of and pushed around by idiots because of this great respectable name of yours—that's what I'm talking about."

"You think you get picked on because of your name?" he asks, as if that isn't what I just said.

"I don't think it. I know it." I'm shouting by this time, and I can feel the edges of my eyes getting wet. I wish he'd just leave already.

"You've sure got your mother's temper," he says, getting up.

"You leave my mother out of this. You're the one with the bad temper, and everyone knows it."

His mouth looks like he bit into something sour again. "Right," he says, and leaves. He closes the door quietly behind him.

17

The Bookshelf

I flop down on the bed, suddenly wiped out. I feel like I'm a can of pop that has exploded, and all that's left are the last few pitiful drops rolling down the side.

I stare at the ceiling for a while, trying to decide what to do next. If I call my mom, she's going to feel guilty for sending me here. She might even cut her vacation short to meet me at home. Of course, it's her fault that I'm here with her grouchy old man; still, I hate to be a baby and ruin her time, too.

It's only four more days. I guess I could stay in this room when he's home and sneak out to get food when he's gone. That way I don't have to see him, plus he'll feel rotten for being such a creep.

If I'm going to stay here, then I'd better find something to do. My sketchpad will help get me through the long hours. The teddy bear doesn't make very good company, and my mother's old bookshelf is the only other thing in the room. I roll off the bed and sit in front of the shelf.

The top row is full of Nancy Drew books and paperbacks. Every one I pick up has a girl on the cover, but I guess I can read a few of them as long as they're mysteries and not romantic junk. The bottom shelf has bigger books on it. There are a couple of school notebooks with my mother's name on the cover and three yearbooks. I find the one with my mother's graduation year and pull it out.

The seniors' pictures are in the front of the book, and they're the only ones that aren't in groups. I flip through the pages of kids in alphabetical order. Lots of them have written "Dear Rita" notes across their faces to say how much they liked her and how she should always remember the good times they had. When I get to the *P*s for Parsons, I can't find my dad. I guess he came to town too late to get his picture in. Mom is easy to find, though. As I get closer to the *S*s, the book falls open to her page, and I spot the teenage Rita Stanislawski. But as I do, a handful of envelopes tumbles into my lap.

It's strange. There are five envelopes. They've all got postmarks, but only one has been opened. The opened one is addressed to Mr. and Mrs. Stanley Stanislawski in loopy handwriting and purple ink. It has a Colorado postmark.

The unopened envelopes are different. They say "S. Stanislawski" in the return corner but are addressed to my mom in Colorado. For some reason, her name and address have been scratched out on each of them, and the words "Return to Sender" have been written. When I realize that the "Return to Sender" message is also written in loopy letters and purple ink, it's like puzzle pieces putting themselves together: My mom refused to read mail that my grandfather sent to her.

I take the handful of letters with me when I leave the room to find my grandfather. He's in the kitchen, sitting at the table, staring out the window. When I pull out the chair across from him and sit down, he looks in my direction.

"I'm sorry," I say. "I shouldn't have yelled."

"Apology accepted," he answers. "I shouldn't have yelled either. I'm sorry, too."

I lay the letters on the table between us. My grandfather picks them up and taps them into a stack. "I see you found my mail."

"I didn't read them," I tell him quickly. "Not even the open one."

"It's an angry letter from your mother, as you might imagine, from when she first left. I was so happy to hear that she was safe, I hardly even minded the things she said in it."

"So you wrote back to her?"

He nods his head. "I wrote to try and bring her back. I told her I was wrong and that the family would work things out if she came back. I still remember what's in those letters because they were so hard for me to write." He taps the stack of letters. "Eventually I quit. It hurt your grandmother too much when one of these would come back unopened." He pulls his lips together for a minute, then starts to talk again. "For years, I left it at that. After Rita came home for her mother's funeral, I started writing again. At least those haven't been returned. That's why I thought it might be time to meet you."

I start to feel sorry for him, then I remember what my mother told me about her leaving. "Why did you hate my dad?" I ask.

My grandfather blows out a long deep breath before he answers. "'Hate' is a strong word, Brad. I didn't *hate* him. I have to admit that I didn't know him well. In a town this small, a new person and the rumors about him get around pretty fast. Before I had even met him, I knew your dad had gotten into trouble in his hometown."

I open my mouth to question him further, but he says, "The kind of trouble isn't the point. He came here to live with an uncle and get straightened out. I assumed he was a troublemaker, and when I found out he was seeing your mother, I went— What's the word they use these days?"

"Ballistic?"

"That's it exactly. I went ballistic. I told her she couldn't see him anymore. Instead of listening, they became more determined to stay together."

My grandfather is quiet for a second, then starts talking softly, almost as if I weren't there to hear him. "I had hoped your mother would be going to college, but she chose your dad instead. To me it looked like she was throwing her life away." He starts talking to me again, pointing to the letters. "As you can see, I tried to make amends, but I was stubborn, too. When she refused my efforts, I gave up."

A person angry enough to refuse letters from her family doesn't seem to have anything to do with the mother I know. "She's not like that now. She's really a good person."

My grandfather smiles. "I'm glad to hear that, but I could already tell. I can see in you what she must be like, and perhaps the kind of person your father was as well. I'm glad to have had the chance to meet you, Brad. You're a great kid."

Hearing him say that makes me feel confused all over again. "You didn't seem to think much of me when I was downstairs with Pat."

My grandfather shakes his head. "I think you just made a mistake. Am I right? You didn't drag that boy in there to peek in the caskets."

"No."

"I wasn't saying you were a bad kid even when I yelled. But I didn't like your behavior, and I expect it to be better from now on."

I nod when he says that. I still don't like it that he chased Pat out, but I'm glad he doesn't hate me. I realize that I don't hate him either.

"Do you think you and Mom will ever be friends again?"

"It's hard to tell," he says. "I had hoped that your visit meant a change of heart on her part, but I'm guessing it was just good timing. Right?"

I feel my face starting to get red.

He keeps talking. "That's all right. Any reason for a visit is better than none. With your mom and me, I'm happy to go one step at a time. Okay?"

"Okay," I say.

He gets up from the table and walks toward my mom's room. I follow him. "While I'm fixing supper," he says, "there's another book that you might enjoy seeing." He picks the yearbook up off the floor, tucks the letters into it, and puts it back on the lower shelf. He scans the upper shelf, moving his hand past the Nancy Drew collection, and pulls out a skinny, leather-covered book and hands it to me.

I don't know how I missed seeing it before. The cover says *Stanislawski the Great: A History.*

18

Stanislawski the Great

I sit at the desk in my mom's room so I can concentrate as I read, but I don't have to force myself. The whole thing is really interesting, and not just because the guy has the same last name as I have.

This Stanislawski was a war hero in Poland. The book is all about his battles and his heroism, the soldiers who loved him, and the townspeople who owed their lives to him. There are black-and-white pictures of his medals and a portrait of the man himself, so I guess it's all true. Before the first chapter, the author put in a page that says Stanislawski the Great was living up to his birthright, since his name means something like "the lord of the manor who becomes worthy of praise."

"Stan-is-lousy" has nothing to do with this guy, that's for sure.

I've finished reading the words under all the pictures

and also a couple of chapters when my grandfather calls to me from the kitchen. I take the book with me and walk out.

There's a glass of milk poured at my place and a cup of tea at my grandfather's. After he takes a tray of pot pies out of the oven and flips one onto each plate, we sit across from each other at the table.

"Is this Stanislawski related to us?" I ask.

He takes the book from me and opens it to the page with the portrait.

"Yes, he is. He was my great-grandfather. Let's see, that would make him your . . ."

"Triple great-grandfather?"

"I guess so."

"He sounds like a pretty big deal."

"Well, he's the most famous Stanislawski, as far as I know. But there are others whose lives were pretty special, too. My grandfather, his son, came to this country not able to speak any English and did well for himself. Eventually, he helped my father open this funeral home."

"I shouldn't have said that stuff about our name," I tell him. I hope I'm all caught up with apologies, since I seem to have owed him a bunch of them.

"It's funny with names. As you get older, you'll find that it's the person who brings pride to his name and not the other way around."

He starts cutting into his food and says, "You know, Mike's taking care of the business tonight. If we don't waste too much time eating, I'll bet we could still get some fishing in this evening. What do you say?"

I chop up my pot pie so it will cool faster, then take a bite from the very edge. "That works for me."

19

Fishing

An hour later, we're in the car on our way to my grandfather's favorite stream. The flies I made are attached to the vest I'll wear. He has his vest, too, the fly box, net, and two rods and reels. "We'll just fish from the bank tonight," he says, "so we won't need wading boots. If you decide you like it, maybe we'll try that another day." We pull off the main road and then bounce along on a stone and dirt road for a while longer. I'm surprised we're so far away from civilization when he stops and says, "I hope you don't mind a bit of walking."

We unload the gear and put on our vests. He leads the way along a winding dirt path. I can hear a stream, but we walk for about ten minutes before we see it.

"This is it," he says. "My favorite stretch of trout waters." We're on a strip of hard-packed dirt, narrower than a sidewalk, that's squeezed between the trees and the water. The stream itself seems to be wide at this point. My grandfather puts our gear down. "Don't go telling everybody about this spot," he says, as if I have anyone to tell. "See that boulder on the other side?"

I nod.

"Well, fish are lazy, just like the rest of us. Given the chance, they prefer places where they don't have to work too hard. The fast water rushes around that big boulder, but the water right behind it is deep and slow. The fish like that. There may not be any fish home tonight, but it would be a good place to start looking."

"Should we cross the stream to get closer?" I ask.

He smiles and shakes his head. "We're not going to catch them with our hands. These rods can increase our reach quite a bit. Let me show you."

He picks up his fly rod and leans it against himself as he tugs a fly off the fuzzy front of his vest. He holds it out for me to see as he attaches it.

"The trees are too close for air casting," he says. "If I swing my line backward before throwing it out, it will just get tangled in the limbs. This is called a roll cast." He holds the rod sideways and flicks it toward the water. His arm hardly moves, but I see the fly enter the stream very close to the boulder.

He holds still for a few seconds, pulls at the line just a little, and waits again. When nothing happens, he draws the line in by hand.

"Can't you just let the fly sit there for a while?"

"That's not the way this game is played." He flicks the line into the water again to almost the same spot. "Real insects move in the water, so should our flies, or they're not going to fool the fish. This isn't the kind of fishing where you sit around with your feet up and take a nap with your line in. A fly fisherman has to keep moving." Once more he uses his hand to bring the line in, then flips it out again.

"Watch my hand this time when I cast," he says.

His finger holds the line still as he brings the rod toward him. As he flicks the rod forward, he lets go at just the right instant, and the line twirls like a whip. Again, the fly lands near the boulder. A second later, my grandfather shouts, "We've got him." He starts working the line with his hand, dragging it in fast. After several handfuls of line have passed by, there's a trout bouncing around at the end. He scoops him up with his net.

My grandfather wraps his hand around the wriggling fish. "This is how we get the little guy unhooked." He draws the hook down and back in the fish's mouth, and it comes loose.

He's still holding the fish, which is flapping its tail hard. "Believe it or not," he says, "I'm not crazy about eating trout, and I really don't care for fixing it. Do you like trout?"

I have no idea, so I just answer, "Not really."

"Okay, we'll give this guy another chance." He eases the fish back into the stream.

"You don't keep them?"

"I haven't for a long time. Your grandmother had a special way to fix trout, and I used to enjoy that a couple of times a year. But even then I threw most of them back. For me, it's all about outsmarting the fish, not killing them."

He picks up the other rod and hands it to me. "Your turn."

20

My Chance at the Fish

I take the fishing rod in my hands. I've been watching carefully, but I still don't know how to start. "I need to put a fly on first, right?" I move the rod from one hand to the other, trying to get one of my flies off my vest. I yank on it and it finally comes loose. As it does, my rod falls to the ground.

My grandfather lays his rod down. "I forget how hard this is when you haven't done it before." He reattaches the fly to my vest. "See?" he says, removing it again. "This is how to get it off. Now you try it." I do, and it's easier this time.

We go through each step that way: He shows me, and I try to repeat it. I learn to put the fly on the end of the leader, and then start to practice casting. Of course that's not as easy as he makes it look either. In fact, I feel like I'm making a video: "Fifty Wrong Ways to Cast a

Fly Line." Camera. Action. Take One: Release my pointer finger from the line too late and cast all of two feet into the water. Take Twelve: Release my pointer finger too early and cast into the weeds behind me. Take Forty-seven: Jerk my arm too hard and send my line a nice long distance, right across my grandfather's line. He stops to untangle us after that one.

"You keep practicing, Brad," he says, moving down the bank. "I'll give you a little more space."

After a while I start to get the hang of it. I don't think about the fish; what I'm doing is target practice. I look at a spot in the stream and try to hit it. I aim for the dark water next to another big rock. My line lands just upstream from where I want it and then moves along on the current. I try to pull it in, but it won't come.

"Hey," I call, "my line's stuck."

My grandfather looks over and sees where it's landed.

"Stuck?" He lays his rod down. "Sure you don't have a bite?"

I pull the line with my hand again. I can move it, but it pulls against me. "Wait. Maybe I do," I shout.

He walks behind me and tells me what to do. "Pull with your left hand. Gently now. Steady. Easy." He holds the net at the surface of the water. "Bring him on in now." Sure enough, there's a wiggling brown trout in the net.

"We need to get this on film," he says, reaching into a

zippered pocket in the back of his vest. "We didn't catch your mother's first fish on film, and I never heard the end of it."

I smile for the camera. Even the fish quits pulling and poses for a second. My grandfather puts the camera back.

"I'll be happy to make this guy for dinner tomorrow, if you want. I make an exception for first fish."

"That's okay," I say. "I'll put him back if you show me how."

He walks me through the steps. I work the fly out of the fish's mouth. I'm about to lay the fish in the water when I lose my grip and he swims away on his own. "I wasn't going to invite you to dinner anyway," I call after him.

My grandfather walks a few feet upstream again. We both start to cast, bring it in, cast again.

I still clamp down on my teeth every time I cast. When my grandfather asks me a question after a few minutes, I'm surprised to find that I can cast and talk at the same time.

"What do you enjoy doing at home? Do you play on any sports teams? Football or anything?"

I hate that question, and people ask it a lot. It's like they think it would give me a good excuse for being big. "No," I say, trying to end that line of questioning.

"I didn't either," he says.

"Really?" I ask. As a kid, he had to have been bigger than average, too. He couldn't have grown this much overnight.

"I tried football for a while. Also basketball. I like watching. I just didn't like playing." He lets out a little laugh. "I forget how old I was when I could admit I wasn't on a team without feeling like I had to apologize. You grow up tall, people have expectations."

"That's for sure," I say.

We fish quietly, then I ask, "Did you get into fights when you were a kid?"

I look over at him, and he seems to be concentrating, but I can't tell if it's on the fish or on my question. Finally he says, "I was luckier than most. I found that I could use my size not to fight."

I cast again, and ask, "How'd you do that?"

He stops fishing and looks my way. "Well, I remember one wise-mouthed kid when I was about your age— maybe even younger. I don't recall what our problem was, but I know every time I saw him he'd say something ugly to make me mad. For a long time I ignored him, but he kept it up. Eventually, I decided I'd had enough."

I bring my line back and raise my rod. "So you beat him up?"

"No," he says. "I was outside one day when he came

around. Whatever he said really set me off. I jumped up, fists clenched at my sides, and told him to knock it off. Right away he was all wide-eyed and apologetic." He reels in his line. "He never bothered me after that. I guess he was just waiting for me to stand up for myself."

I try to picture my grandfather as a boy yelling at the kid, but I can't do it. When I do make him look young in my mind, the kid I see is me.

It's getting dark, so we gather our fishing gear and start up the path toward the car. The fireflies are coming out now. I've seen them in books, but being this close to them is better than I imagined. I nearly trip a couple of times watching their tiny yellow-green glowlights twinkle as I walk. Fireflies weren't on my See It This Summer list, but I think they should have been. Even palm trees couldn't be this cool.

"Tomorrow morning," he says as we reach the car, "I'll be going over to the church to help set up for the bazaar. Want to come?"

"Sure," I say, and we two fishermen ride back home.

21

Getting Ready for the Festival

In the morning, my grandfather stops in the funeral home to talk with Mike before we go to the church. He flips through the sign-in book at the entrance to the room where Mrs. Mihalko is. "Looks like you were pretty busy last night," he says. "Did all of the out-of-town family get in yet?"

"I think a few of them are still coming this afternoon," Mike answers. He turns to me and asks, "So you're going to help set up for the Saint Mary's festival?"

"Yep," I nod.

"Well, have a good time. With any luck, I can get up there tomorrow night."

"See you later, Mike. Page me if you need anything," my grandfather says, and we go to the car.

"If Mike goes to the festival, does that mean you can't?" I ask him.

"Not unless we get another business call."

When we pull into the church parking lot, there are several cars and a couple of pickup trucks already there. People say hi to my grandfather just like they did at the baseball game. He introduces me to some of them. Mosorjak. Surkosky. Strybel. Gorecki. As we walk across the churchyard where no one can hear us, I tell him, "I've never heard of most of these names."

My grandfather laughs. "I can't help it if you don't live in a good Polish neighborhood. I imagine you have a few names out your way that I'm not familiar with."

"Is everyone in Wallace Corners Polish?"

"Not even close," he says. "But a lot of the people who go to Saint Mary's are, or their grandparents were. When the coal mines were still running, workers came from all over Europe, one country at a time."

"So they each had their own church?"

"It's not as if they stopped other people from joining, but each group did build its own. If you were here next month for the Saint Michael's festival, almost every name you'd hear would be Italian. You missed the Hungarian festival over Memorial Day."

We reach a group of men and women standing near a big stack of wood that looks like giant, double-layered picture frames. Several other people are carrying more pieces out of a storage shed. "Hi, Stanley," one man says. "Did you bring us some help?"

"Yes. Greg, this is my grandson, Brad."

"Hi," I say, shaking his hand.

"Well, grab hold on the other side, gentlemen." Greg points to one of the frames. He lifts one side of the heavy frame while my grandfather and I lift the other. We walk across the churchyard. "I think this is about where we had Chuck-O-Luck last year," Greg says, lowering his side of the frame to the ground. We follow his lead, but I still have no clue what we're doing. I notice my grandfather is breathing hard as we go back to the pile and get another. When we put the second frame near the first, he pulls out a handkerchief and wipes his forehead.

"You okay, Stanley?" Greg asks.

"Sure," he says. "What's next?"

"We need to lift this. Brad, you balance it while your grandpa and I attach the next piece."

They put several boards and hinges into place, and I hold things where they tell me to. In a couple of minutes, we've built a booth. They tie a plastic sheet with the numbers one to six across a shelf in the front and hang a wheel on the back wall.

Greg smiles in my direction. "You'll have to try your luck here tomorrow night. It's a scientific fact that you do best at the booths you help to build."

Another friend of Greg's joins us. When he does, my grandfather says, "If you men can handle this, I'd better see how the cooks are doing." He starts toward the church basement door.

"It's starting to smell pretty good in there," Greg calls after him.

Greg, his friend, and I keep building booths while other people are doing the same. Pretty soon, the frame pile is gone.

"Is there something else you need help with?" I ask Greg, even though my arms and back are getting tired.

"We've got it under control out here. Why don't you track down your grandpa?"

As I walk toward the church basement, I hear someone call from the sidewalk. "Hey, Brad." It's Pat Robinson on his bike. I walk over to him.

"So, you escaped the old creep?"

My eyes dart to the church basement. I hope my grandfather isn't close enough to hear us.

"Don't say that," I tell him. "He's here someplace."

Pat raises his voice louder. "Of course, he's here someplace. You didn't think he was going to let you out of his sight, did you? Now that you've had some fun?"

"Listen," I say quietly, "I've got to go. Maybe I'll see you later."

I turn to leave, but he calls after me. "Let me know if the old coot takes off. Maybe we can do some more exploring."

Luckily, my grandfather must still be inside. As I walk toward the church basement, the smell of food gets stronger. There's something spicy cooking. I smell baking, too.

It takes my eyes a minute to get used to the lack of sun when I first walk in. There are lots of voices, most of them women's, coming from somewhere in the back. I walk toward the noise and find a kitchen crowded with workers. My grandfather is talking to an older woman in an apron. She's putting two small bags and a couple of big jars into a paper grocery bag.

"You're spoiling me, Stella. You'd better save some of this food for the weekend."

The lady laughs and puts in the last jar. "You just be sure to lose an extra dollar or two at bingo, and it will come out even," she says.

My grandfather sees me, introduces us, and gets ready to leave. The woman scoots up behind me with a smaller paper bag. "This is just for you, honey," she says. "You don't have to share it."

"Thanks."

As we leave, I ask my grandfather, "What is all this?"

"Stella Boroski is the best Polish cook I know now that your grandmother has passed away. This," he says, holding up the bag, "is dinner."

Later, as we finish the food Mrs. Boroski sent, I feel sorry for my grandfather and his freezer full of frozen food. This stuff is a whole lot different, and I can tell he really likes it. Most of what she sent was *halupki*, which he says is also called pigs in the blanket. They serve pigs in the blanket at my school, but there it's just a biscuit wrapped around a hot dog. Mrs. Boroski's *halupki* doesn't have either of those in it. There's cabbage in hers, which is why I'm surprised that I like it. The cabbage is the blanket, and the pig is a mixture of meat and rice. It's all cooked in tomato juice. She also put in some pieces of Polish sausage, but I don't care much for that.

"What did you get in your secret bag, Brad?" my grandfather asks.

I open it and pull out three fat, rolled-up cookies about the size of my thumb.

"Nut rolls," he says. "You're going to like those."

"Here, do you want one?"

"Didn't you hear Mrs. Boroski? You'd better eat them all. She'll check that you did."

I do, and I wonder afterward if I'll still be able to move by the time the weekend is over. After all, the festival hasn't even started.

22

St. Mary's Festival

Friday is the day the festival starts. Mike and my grandfather are tied up with Mrs. Mihalko's funeral early in the day. I run a couple of errands, then hang around the house. In the newspaper, I notice a picture of the Pirates' best hitter. I know my grandfather likes the team, so I get out my sketchbook and turn the guy into a baseball superhero. His shoulders are hard to draw, so I work on them for a long time. I add huge, bulging muscles on his arms and calves, and a look on his face that says he's ready to hit one out of the park.

My grandfather comes in just about the time I'm finishing. He looks at the picture and smiles. "You sure do good work, but there's something missing."

"What?" I ask.

"You need to sign it. Every artist's work ought to be signed."

I write my name at the bottom, tear the sheet off the sketchpad, and hand it to him. He leans it against some framed pictures on top of the TV. I'm surprised that I feel more proud than embarrassed when he puts it there.

It's early in the evening when my grandfather and I head up to the festival. We haven't eaten supper yet. "Those ladies have worked hard getting that food ready. The least we can do is buy some," he says with a chuckle.

The parking lot at the church is almost full as we pull in, and some people have parked on the street as well. Everything seems different than it did yesterday. There's music coming from the basement, but there must be speakers outside, too, since the sound seems to be every-where. The booths we built are lined up in the yard, and people are gathering at all of them. At the end, there's a big striped tent with open sides and lots of tables under-neath. A bingo caller is speaking into a microphone, "I-twenty-four. That's twenty-four under the *I*." Between the other booths and the bingo tent, someone is selling pop, but I can tell from the smell that most of the food is being served in the basement.

"Let's get something to eat," my grandfather says as we walk toward the open basement door.

Inside it's noisier than it is on the lawn. At one end of the hall, a band is setting up. The music that's already playing must be coming from a CD player. It's not the kind of stuff you hear on the radio. I know from music class that an accordion is one of the instruments I'm hearing. A couple of grown-ups and some little kids are on the dance floor, but most of the people are in a buffet line outside the kitchen.

The *halupki* they made yesterday is there, and many other choices as well. "I'll bet you'll want to try some goulash," my grandfather says, handing me a paper plate for the stew. He spoons some pillowy things, like ravioli, on his plate and says, "Does your mom ever make *pierogi*? She used to love them stuffed with mashed potatoes."

"No. I don't think I've ever eaten these." I put a couple on my plate.

As we get to the sweets, there are even more choices. "I would highly recommend a pineapple bar," Grandpa says, "and some of this Polish pastry. It's called *chrusciki*." He's pointing to fried dough strips with powdered sugar. "Just like doughnuts, only better," he adds.

Grandpa pays for the food, and we carry our plates to one of the long tables.

"Nice to see you, Mr. Stanislawski," a woman says when we sit down across from her family. She points to the man beside her and says, "You remember my husband, Tom. And I don't think you've met Anne and

Benny." She points to her kids. The boy is a messy-faced toddler. The girl is about my age.

"Hi, Tom." Grandpa shakes the man's hand. "This is my grandson, Brad. He's from Colorado."

I nod to say hi.

The mom gets so excited, you would have thought my grandfather had said, "He's from Africa."

"I've always wanted to go out West, haven't I, Tom? My sister drove through Colorado on her way to California two years ago. She said she never saw such a pretty place, with the mountains and all." She takes a breath, and then adds, "How long have you lived there?"

"All my life." Then, just to be cute, I add, "So far."

The woman looks surprised. She asks my grandfather, "Has Rita been gone that long?"

He plunks a forkful of food into his mouth and just nods.

Her husband changes the subject to how the Pirates have been playing, and we eat the meal without any more questions.

I finish my food (the mashed-potato pillows and the powdered sugar dough are my new favorites) and get ready to throw the paper plate away, when the mom grabs it from me. "I'll take those." She takes my grandfather's, too. "Anne, why don't you and Brad try a polka before you go outside?"

Anne smiles a little, but just shrugs her shoulders. "You want to?"

I look to my grandfather for help, but he's not offering any. "Go ahead. I'll wait here."

This would be a great time to practice saying no to people, but I don't. I get up and start walking toward the dance floor. Anne comes from around the table and joins me. I feel better when I see that the floor is more crowded now. At least I won't stick out as much.

"Do you know how to polka?" Anne asks.

"No. This probably isn't a good idea."

"It's easy." She takes my left hand in her right, and puts my other arm around her waist. "It's just one, two, three, one, two, three." I look down at her sneakers. "One, two, three, one, two, three," she repeats as she moves her feet.

I try to imitate her for a few steps, but it feels awkward.

"It's easier when you go fast, like the music," she says.

"Oh." I hadn't even been listening to the music. I take my eyes off her feet long enough to see pairs of people one-two-threeing in fast forward. Some of them have spins and kicks added in. A man as old as my grandfather adds a little yelp as he dances by.

"What the heck." I look back at her feet. "Let's go."

By the time "Roll Out the Barrel" is over, I'm not having a barrel of fun like the song says, but I haven't fallen or tripped anyone. That's something.

"You want to try another one?" Anne asks.

"Maybe later," I say and walk back toward the table. "Thanks for teaching me."

"Ready to head outside?" my grandfather asks, getting up.

I am, but I just nod and keep my mouth shut. My stomach doesn't like dancing the polka after eating *pierogi* any more than it liked landing in an airplane.

23

Trying Our Luck

It's still daylight when we come out of the church basement, but strings of lights are glowing around all the booths. It's also more crowded now.

"I hope you didn't mind your polka lesson too much," my grandfather says. "I just figured that a boy named Stanislawski should know how, and I would have looked pretty silly out there trying to teach you."

"I'll get over it." When I hear how that sounds, I add, "It wasn't too bad."

We walk to the stuffed animal booth. "Want to try some tip seals?" he asks. He hands the lady in charge a couple of dollars, then he reaches into a big jar and takes out a handful of tickets. "You pull ten from the other jar," he tells me.

The tickets are small folded number strips, sealed shut with a paper band. When I bend it back like a fortune cookie, the paper band breaks and I unfold it.

"Anything ending in two zeroes or a fifty is a winner," the lady says.

My grandfather and I go through all our tickets, but neither of us wins. Actually, I'm sort of glad I didn't. I don't feel like carrying a stuffed animal around.

We try a couple of other tip seal booths, one with artificial flowers as prizes and the other with kitchen things. At the kitchen booth, one of my tickets is a 1250. The man matches my number to the prize, and we leave there with a red-and-white-checked tablecloth.

"I might have to wrestle you for that," my grandfather says.

"I just might let you win," I say, laughing.

We don't stop to toss nickels to win glasses or throw darts for Barbie dolls. "Let's see if we can win something more useful," my grandfather says. "Money." We walk in the direction of the Chuck-O-Luck booth.

Chuck-O-Luck is the most popular game at the festival. People of all ages are crowded there. I get close enough to watch.

"Get your money down. Money down," a man calls as he spins the giant dial. Nickels, dimes, and quarters sit on the counter numbers. The wheel's numbers look like dice, and each slot of the wheel has three of them.

The wheel slowly comes to a stop. "That's an ace, a three, and a four," the man says. Quickly, his helper matches coin for coin on the one, three, and four squares. He collects the money from the other squares.

"Money down," the man says again. People slap it down fast. I guess you're not allowed to sneak it on at the last minute. "Six, six, deuce," the man says when the wheel stops. The payout guy matches two coins for each one sitting on number six. The coins on the two get paid once. Everyone else loses.

"Ready to try your luck?" my grandfather says, laying one quarter on the three and another on the six.

I pull two dimes out of my pocket and put them both on the one.

"Ace, three, five," the wheel man says.

"Hey, this is all right," I say, collecting the two extra dimes.

"Money down," the man says. We lay our coins on the board.

Just then, Mike comes up behind us. "So, are you winning?" he asks.

"Three fours!" the wheel man calls. The payout guy scoops our money away.

"No," we say together, and smile.

"Money down," the man calls, and we place our coins. This time, my grandfather wins on two squares, but Mike and I lose. The next three times the man spins the wheel, my grandfather wins again.

"Did you ever see anyone as lucky as this guy?" Mike says. "I wonder if he shouldn't quit the funeral business and become a full-time gambler."

I expect to hear my grandfather laugh at that, but he just says, "I think I'm ready for a break," and takes a step back from the booth. He looks kind of serious for someone who's been cleaning up at Chuck-O-Luck. "I'm going to sit in the bingo tent."

"I'll come with you," I say. "Just wait until this next spin," but he's already heading across the grass.

"Four, four, two," the man calls.

I grab the two dimes that the man lays next to the one I have on the number four, and stuff them in my pocket. "Wait up," I call. But he doesn't answer.

I turn around just in time to see my grandfather collapse onto the grass.

21

The Hospital

"Give him some room!" a man yells, as he and a woman who seem to know what they're doing roll my grandfather onto his back. Half the people at the festival have suddenly swooped to the place where my grandfather fell. The hospital is just across the street, and someone must have called for help because the ambulance comes right away. From where I'm stuck in the crowd, I can barely make out my grandfather's pantleg and ankle as they load him on the stretcher. No one realizes that he was with me. I open my mouth as I crane to see, but no noise comes out.

The ambulance pulls away. As it does, bystanders stare after it. They stand still at first, then cluster into groups where I hear voices saying, "Poor Stush," and "I didn't know he was ill." Before long, they start going back to their games and food. The music from the basement has been playing all along. The bingo caller starts again.

Pat Robinson must have been in the crowd. As the people move away, I see him out of the corner of my eye. He walks close to where I've been standing frozen and says, "Too bad about the old grouch. I wonder who takes care of the stiff if the stiff is the undertaker?"

His words smack me awake from the stupor I've been in. Without thinking, I turn and make a flying tackle in his direction. If he had had a second to move out of my path, I would have gotten a face full of grass. Instead, I make a direct hit and get a face full of Pat Robinson.

On top of him on the ground, I've got Pat's shoulders in my hands. I shake him hard and yell, "Take it back," over and over again.

It seems like I've been screaming for a while when I feel my shirt and shoulders being pulled back.

"Brad," someone yells. "Let him up."

It's Mike. I let go of Pat and roll off him. He scrambles to his feet, and yells, "Nut case!" I don't see his face, but I hear him suck in a noseful of snot. I bet he's crying.

Mike gives me a hand, and I get up. "I was looking for you. What was that all about?" he asks.

"My grandfather. Pat said . . . ," and then I can't finish it. I feel the tears rush up in my eyes and nose. When I suck it in, I sound as loud as Pat did.

"Let's go home. You can wash up, then we'll go to the hospital and check on him," he says. "How's that?"

I nod, and we leave the lights of the Saint Mary's festival behind us.

Mike calls the hospital while I wash and change clothes. I feel better when I come out, but worse all over again when he says, "He's in intensive care, but we can go up for a few minutes. I think I can get you in."

I know all about intensive care. That's where funeral directors go to pick up the dead.

"We need to call your mom, too," Mike says.

"They don't talk," I tell him.

"We'll still need to call her. But it can wait until we get back." He puts his arm around my shoulder. "Ready?" he asks.

When we get to intensive care, the nurse comes to the door to meet us. "He's stable right now," she says quietly. "The doctors have ordered some tests, so we'll know more in the morning." Then she adds, "You can come in for a few minutes, but he's sleeping."

We walk into the room. It's a good thing the nurse knows who we've come to see because it would take me a while to find him. There are people in six of the beds, but the tubes and wires make them all look alike. Only their hair and size make them different. My grandfather is the largest lump under the covers, but even he looks a lot smaller than usual. The machines he's connected to seem like they are pumping stuff out of him instead of in.

Mike and I stand beside his bed. I try not to notice what a terrible color his face is. It reminds me of the way Mrs. Mihalko's looked that night we came here to get her. Instead, I concentrate on watching his chest move up and down.

We've been there only a few minutes when Mike tells me, "We'd better be going."

As if that's my grandfather's cue, he opens his eyes and smiles. In a groggy voice he says, "Hi, guys. What's up?" He waves the fingers on the hand that doesn't have any tubes attached to it.

It's such a relief to hear him talk. "Grandpa" is all I can say. I move closer to the bed and lean down to hug him. It's not easy, since I have to dodge the tubes.

The nurse comes over then. "How are you feeling, Mr. Stanislawski?"

"Better now." But he adds, "I'm going to close my eyes for a minute," and he's asleep again.

"Come on," Mike says, and we leave.

Back at the funeral home Mike tells me he'll stay here tonight. We can figure out what to do tomorrow after we talk to the doctors.

"You should probably call your mom, though, just in case. Let her know we'll call again in the morning."

I find the number my mom has given me for her hotel and close the door of Grandpa's office behind me. She answers on the third ring.

"Brad, I was just thinking about you. I'm getting ready to go out with David, and I was going to call you before I left." She takes a breath and then says, "So what's up?"

"Grandpa had some kind of attack at the church festival. He's in the hospital."

"Gosh, are you okay? Is anyone with you now?"

I close my eyes tight and take a deep breath. I don't remember ever lying to my mom, but I'm about to break that record with a whopper. "No," I say, trying to keep my voice steady. "Mike is out of town. I'm not sure when he'll be back."

"Oh, good heavens. I wish your father's people still lived around there. I don't know who else to have you call."

"I'm fine, Mom, but I hope you can come soon."

"I'll fly out first thing in the morning, honey. Don't worry. Just make sure all the doors are locked and keep as many lights on in the house as you want." I can tell by her voice she's just now picturing where I am. "There isn't a— Your grandfather wasn't busy at the funeral home, was he?"

"No," I tell her, glad that that at least is the truth.

I need to get off the phone before I break down and

become a completely honest person again. "Listen, Mom, I have to go now. I'm fine. Really," I answer her. "I love you, too. Good-bye."

I open the office door. Mike calls, "It's about time to head in, isn't it?" but I'm already on my way. I feel like I've been up for days.

It's a relief to be in bed with the lights off. As soon as I close my eyes, though, my mind starts messing with everything that happened today. I'm spinning around, doing the polka in the church basement. Everything else flashes by fast: My grandfather plays Chuck-O-Luck. My grandfather lies on the ground. My grandfather is in the hospital bed, hooked up to machines. I spin so fast that I fall, too. I look up from the floor and Pat Robinson is standing over me. Anthony from Colorado is beside him. "Hey, Stan-is-lousy," Pat says, "who takes care of the stiff?" "Yeah," Anthony says, "who takes care of the stiff if the stiff is the undertaker?" Both of them laugh. Then suddenly, they disappear and Mike is there. I'm happy to see him until he says, "We'll call your mother. Just in case."

The last thing I remember from my dream is looking up at Mike and saying, "What do you mean, just in case?"

"You know," he says. "In case he dies."

25

Visitors

I open my eyes in the morning and feel the same weird where-am-I? feeling that I had on my first day here. I'm at my grandfather's house, I tell myself, and then I remember: my grandfather isn't.

I get dressed and go to the kitchen. There's a note on the table from Mike. *I'm working in the office. Let me know when you get up.*

The office door is open, but Mike has his back turned to me. He's sitting at the desk, talking on the phone. His voice sounds serious. A huge knot hits my stomach when I hear what he's saying.

"You're moving him out then? So where will I find him?" He starts writing on a notepad. "All right. I'll be there soon. Thanks." He hangs up.

Mike starts to stand when he sees me. He looks surprised. "Well, good morning. I just talked to the hospital. I have to go up there in a few minutes."

Get to the point, I want to tell him. *I know why you're going to the hospital.* I don't mean to, but when I open my mouth, I blurt out, "He's dead, isn't he?"

"Dead?" he says, and then smiles. "No. They just called with good news. They decided to move him out of intensive care because he's doing a lot better. In fact, he should be able to come home in a few days."

My fingernails have been digging into the palms of my hands. I feel my fingers starting to relax.

"Get some breakfast," he says. "Then we can go up together."

The room Mike leads us to is in a whole different part of the hospital from intensive care. We walk in and see two beds in my grandfather's room. He's in the one by the window. I don't know what kind of juice they were feeding him last night, but it must have been powerful stuff. He looks like my grandfather again.

"Hey, Brad," he says. He even sounds like himself. "How's my favorite grandson?"

"I'm fine." I walk closer. "How are you?"

"Better than I was yesterday. It was looking like I had a heart attack, but now they're pretty sure I didn't."

"That's great," I say. "So what was the matter?"

"Oh, my heartbeats were all out of whack. I'll need medication to fix that, and, of course, they want to run a few more tests while I'm here. But it doesn't seem too serious."

"It's good to see you looking better," Mike says, shaking his hand. I wonder if I'll shake hands all the time when I'm his age.

"Mike," my grandfather says, "the doctor is telling me to slow down a bit. You and I should probably talk business when I get out of here."

"That's fine with me," Mike answers. "Whenever you're ready."

"Why don't you pull those chairs over here and sit a while?" he suggests, and we do.

My grandfather tells Mike about my dancing the polka in the church basement and says he thinks I've got that "Stanislawski charm." Mike doesn't tell my grandfather about my jumping Pat Robinson. I'm thinking that I might later, though. Since nobody got hurt, he probably won't be mad, but I'd like to ask him what he would have done.

By the time we've been there a few minutes, they're talking about how the Pirates have been playing. It's almost as if nothing ever happened.

"Hey, Brad," Mike says, "we'd better go and call your mother. We can come back later." We tell my grandfather good-bye and hurry out.

I know there's no point in calling my mother, but Mike doesn't. I dial the hotel and of course she's already checked out. My stomach tightens when I realize she's in an airplane right now because I lied and said I was alone. It's probably not the smartest thing I've ever done.

"Well," Mike says. "I guess we messed that up." He looks at his watch. "It's still early in California. She must have been really worried."

"Yeah," I answer, but I don't tell him I'm the one she was worried about.

He takes some money out of his wallet. "If I go back to my place for a while, would you check that there will be some food for your mom when she gets here? Just make sure there's milk, that sort of thing."

"Okay."

He picks up his car keys, ready to leave.

"What time does the church festival start today?" I ask.

"What is this, Saturday? I suppose they'll be open this afternoon. Why?"

"I thought my mom might like some *halupki* for dinner. Her mom used to make it."

"Sounds like a plan." Then Mike laughs. "But don't lose all the money at Chuck-O-Luck before you can buy some."

I make a quick run to the store and then to the festival. It's a lot quieter there today, but the ladies are still cooking and selling food. Mrs. Boroski remembers me from the other day and asks about my grandfather. Apparently, everyone knows about last night. "Mr. Stanislawski is the nicest man," she says. "I'm so glad to hear that he's already starting to feel better." She puts in a handful of nut rolls and doesn't charge me for them. "You tell him all the ladies at the church asked about him, won't you?"

Back at the house, I straighten things up the way Mom always does when she has friends over. I figure it's the least I can do. To take my mind off my crimes, I spend the rest of the afternoon drawing. I've about perfected my seven-toed, dragon-winged monster when my mom walks in.

"Hey, sweetie," she says, pulling me in for a big hug. She's shorter than I am, but she can pack a lot of muscle into her hugs. This one almost folds me in half, but I don't mind. I didn't realize how much I've missed her. After a couple of kisses on the cheek, she lets me go.

"How was your trip?" I ask.

"Not bad. We were actually a few minutes early getting into Pittsburgh."

"Not that trip," I say. "California. Did you swim in the ocean? Did you see palm trees? Did you visit Disneyland?"

"Yes, yes, and no," she says. "But I'll tell you all about that later. I want to know how you're doing. I hope you weren't afraid last night."

"No," I say. I know Mike will be back soon, so it's time to tell the truth. "I wasn't by myself after all."

She looks confused and sits down hard in my grandfather's chair. I land on the arm of the couch.

"Mike came back?" she asks.

I could probably get away with that story, but I'm ready to retire from my short career as a liar. "No, Mom. He was going to be here all along."

"Then why would you say that he wasn't?"

"Because Grandpa seemed really sick, and I figured you wouldn't come to see him otherwise."

"You're right. I wouldn't have." She looks both tired and mad. "You know, it's not like I wasn't straight with you before you came out here. I told you how he hurt me. Why would you do this?"

Without answering, I get up and walk to my mom's bedroom, get the letters out of the yearbook, and take them back to the living room.

"This is why." I hand them to her. "You hurt him, too."

She tosses the letters to the table beside her as if they're hot. "Brad, he all but kicked me out of the house! Then after I left, he sent his anger after me in letters. I refused to let him continue badgering me, that's all. Why are you saying *I* hurt *him*? Returning them unopened was just self-defense."

When I lied to make my mom come, I thought it would fix everything. So much for my brilliant scheme. But since I'm this far into the mess, I put my nose in her business once more. "Mom," I say quietly, "why don't you just read the letters?"

"This is better left in the past." She shakes her head as if she's disgusted with herself. "I don't know what I was thinking, sending you here."

I reach over and grab her hand. "It's important, Mom. Just read them, okay?"

Her eyes pinch shut. I can't tell if she's trying to shut out me or her past. She opens her eyes a minute later and picks up one of them.

As she reads, I sit on the couch, staring toward the window. When she opens the second letter, I go to get myself a drink of water in the kitchen, taking my time before I go back in. I hear her sniffle as she starts reading the third one, so I take a glass of water to her, too. By the time she finishes the last letter, she's calmed down.

She stares at the letters for a minute, then looks at me. "You're right, of course. He was trying to make amends. So I did hurt him. And my mother, too. She would have helped put our family back together if I'd have let her." My mom smiles a little and adds, "In case you haven't noticed, bullheadedness is not this family's most endearing quality."

"Mom," I say, "you're not like that anymore. You're a great mom."

She smiles at me, and I can see tears in her eyes.

"And Grandpa isn't either," I tell her. "You'll like him."

"How is he?" she asks.

"He was a lot better this morning. They took him out of intensive care."

She pulls a tissue out of her pants pocket and blows her nose. She clears her voice and then says, "None of this gave you permission to lie to me."

"I know that. I'm sorry. Really."

"But I'm glad I'm here. I'll put my stuff away, then you can take me to the hospital."

Half an hour later, I walk into the hospital room. My grandfather's eyes are closed, but he opens them as I get near the bed. Right away, he smiles.

"Grandpa," I say, "I've brought someone to see you."

26

A Family Reunion

My mom walks into the room, wrapping her arms around herself as if she's suddenly cold. "Hi, Dad," she says quietly.

"Rita" is all Grandpa answers.

She walks up to the bed slowly, but two seconds later they're locked in this huge bear hug. It may be that Mom learned her hugging skills from my grandfather, since she's the one who ends up nearly folded in half this time.

They both look wet-eyed when they're finished, but my grandfather hides this by blowing his nose. Neither of them says anything, so I do. "Pull up a chair, Mom. Sit down." I hope I don't have to keep being the adult here. It wears me out.

Once we sit, Mom and Grandpa start to talk. "How are you feeling?" my mom asks.

Grandpa sounds kind of formal when he answers, like

she's someone he just met. "Much better, thanks. Did you enjoy your vacation?"

"Yes," she says, sounding just as stiff. "It was wonderful."

Everybody is quiet for a minute, then my mom starts in again.

"I hear you still have a knack for teaching fly fishing. Sounds like Brad really enjoyed himself."

"He can tie, too. Did he show you his flies yet?" he asks, looking at me.

"She just got here. I'll show her as soon as we get back."

"He's already caught a nice-sized brownie on a nymph that he tied himself," he says.

They go on talking about me and fishing for a while. Then they move on to me and drawing. I could get big-headed over all the compliments I'm hearing, but I have a feeling I'm the topic just because I'm what they both know about.

After we've been there a while, I offer to go and buy everyone a soda at the coffee shop. I walk through the hospital waiting area to get there.

"Hey," a voice says as I pass the rows of chairs and magazines. I look up to see Pat Robinson. Judging by the flaming red hair of the woman in the seat beside him, I'd say he's with his mother.

My brain races back to the last time I saw him, brushing the dirt off himself at the church festival. It feels like weeks ago, but it's been less than twenty-four hours. I hope he isn't here because of anything I did to him. My guilty conscience drags me over to them. Pat is holding his right arm with his left one.

"What's up?" I say.

Pat's mother talks before he has a chance. "He fell from a ladder that he had no business being on in the first place. Something about bird-watching?"

Pat catches my eye and nods just a little. "You know, like we were doing the other day? Bird-watching?"

"Right." It's tempting to say, *You mean when we were trying to break into that vacant house?* but I don't. He's already gotten a hurt arm out of whatever happened to him today. There's no point in my making it worse.

I shift my weight from one foot to the other, ready to move on. "Well," I say, "I'd better get going."

"How's your grandfather?" Pat asks. There's no wise-guy sound in his voice, no mention of the word *stiff.*

"I think he's going to be fine. I hope your arm feels better," I add, and head off again to the coffee shop.

A few minutes later, as I pass them on my way back, Pat's mother has her arm around him, but she still looks annoyed as they talk. I guess I'm lucky we weren't hanging out together today.

When I reach the hall outside my grandfather's room, I can hear that I'm not the subject of conversation anymore. My grandmother is. Mom's the one blowing her nose this time. Then my grandfather says something that makes her laugh. That's my cue to take the drinks in, and we all talk some more.

Mom and Grandpa have a lot to catch up on. He tells her about Wallace Corners and some people she used to know. She tells him about her work in real estate and about her friends in Denver. They never even get around to discussing how the Pirates are playing. After a while, the nurse, who has already been in a few times to take my grandfather's pulse, brings him some pills in a cup.

"I have your medication, Mr. Stanislawski," she announces loudly.

He swallows the stuff she gives him and hands the cup back.

"It will make him drowsy," the nurse tells us quietly. I guess that's a polite way of saying it's time to go home, so we do.

My grandfather has to stay in the hospital until his tests are finished, so I'm glad Mom is here. I wouldn't want Mike to feel like a baby-sitter for me.

She and I visit the festival before it closes on Sunday. More than once someone stops her and says, "Is that you, Rita?" After a minute of looking confused, my mother's face breaks into a smile and, depending on who the person is, hugs or handshakes follow. As we walk away, she tells me "That girl was the funniest person in our whole school" or "I had a crush on that boy from the time I was in sixth grade." It's good to see her enjoying herself, so I don't mention that the words *girl* and *boy* don't really fit the chubby woman or the man who's almost bald.

27

Going Home

On Tuesday, my grandfather is released from the hospital. After Mom drives him home, we all go into the living room. "Can I get you something to drink, Dad? A Coke or some coffee?" Mom asks.

"No, thanks," he says.

"Do you want me to fluff up that pillow behind your back?" I add.

Grandpa puts up with us for about ten seconds.

"You two will drive me crazy if I let you," he says, with a fake kind of rough voice. "What I need is a little time on a trout stream. Care to join me?"

Mom looks surprised and opens her mouth like she's going to object, but she closes it again without saying anything. A few seconds later, she gets off the couch, smiles, and says, "I'll have to change clothes first. Give me a minute."

I follow her out of the room. "Are you sure this is a good idea?" I whisper. "We had to walk a long way when he took me fishing the other day."

But Mom doesn't look a bit worried. "I still remember a thing or two about this grandpa of yours. Fishing is his best medicine." She smiles and strokes my cheek. "Don't worry. We won't let him exert himself."

It takes us a while to help Grandpa gather the gear, but he's got enough rods and reels for all of us. Mom fills her arms with the equipment and starts downstairs.

"Take it easy on the steps, you two," she calls over her shoulder.

I take that as a signal to offer Grandpa my arm as we follow her. He seems steady enough on his feet, which is a good thing, since I'm not sure I could hold him if he fell.

After Mom helps Grandpa into the passenger seat, she gets in. "Where to, Dad?"

"Let's just go out to Sandy Creek."

Without any more instructions, she knows where to drive us. We ride for twenty minutes on winding roads, then she parks the car. The water is close by, and soon we're all casting into the stream.

My mom stands a bit downstream from Grandpa, and I'm just below her. From my spot on the bank, I can see them both as I cast my line. Mom's first few casts look as bad as mine did the other day. But before long, her line sails into the water just like Grandpa's. She even knows how to look for the fish by the big rocks. When she gets a tug on her line, she starts to holler loud enough that the poor fish is probably terrified. "Dad! Brad! I've got one on!" Sure enough, she reels in a beautiful rainbow trout.

We catch five among us before we're finished, and we leave with a roll of film full of smiles and fish.

The rest of the week goes by fast. Grandpa looks less tired and more like himself each day. He spends lots of time with us and some working in his office. A business call comes in about nine o'clock Friday night, but he phones Mike to take care of the hospital pickup. Mom says she's glad to see him easing up a little.

On Saturday, it's time to fly home. I'm just zipping my second duffel bag when Grandpa knocks on the doorframe. Holding up a Ziploc bag, he says, "Do you suppose you could find some room in there for a couple of 'scalps'?"

"That would be great." I take the bag and tuck it into the middle of my clothes, where it shouldn't get damaged.

"That's a bit of hare and some turkey neck for feathers. There's a box of hooks inside, too, and a little cash so that, if you decide to give fly-tying a try, you can buy yourself a vise."

"Thanks, Grandpa."

"Of course, I don't know much about the trout streams out West. You'll have to experiment at first. You might keep an eye out for people who know what they're doing."

"Maybe after I learn some things, I can teach you when you come to visit," I offer.

My grandfather smiles and nods, then pulls me in for one of those long, famous Stanislawski hugs.

On the way downstairs with the bags, we stop to see Mike in the funeral home. "I sure enjoyed meeting you, Brad," he says, shaking my hand. "And you, too, Rita. I hope you're planning to come back soon."

"Maybe next summer," my mom answers. "Or who knows? Maybe Dad will come out our way instead. How about convincing him that this place could run for a few days without him?"

"I'll do my best," Mike says.

It's funny, but saying good-bye to Grandpa reminds me of saying hello to him at the airport. "Don't eat too much on the plane," he tells me. "You might get an upset stomach."

I nod. "I'll be fine."

"Be sure to watch when I'm on the game show, Dad," Mom tells him.

"I won't forget," he answers. "But call and remind me anyway."

After a few more hugs and kisses, we finally get into the car. "I'll phone you when we get home," Mom says.

"I'll be here." Grandpa takes a few steps back from the car and puts a hand in his pocket. "Drive carefully."

He waves and smiles with his mouth closed tight. I'm guessing he'll be blowing his nose again before we reach the corner. It's one more thing we have in common.

28

Showdown

The airplane trip is fine. Mom and I sit in different sections of the plane, since we bought our tickets separately, but I don't mind. I like the idea of traveling alone. It gives me a chance to think about things.

The landing is only slightly easier than it was the first time. This flying stuff is harder than it looks. There's no doubt about it: I'd rather be a cartoonist than a pilot.

Colorado looks as strange to me as Pennsylvania did when I first got there. The sun is bright, and the sky appears to be huge, but it feels like there aren't enough trees. When we pull up to our house, the automatic lawn sprinklers are running. My grandfather's lawn was bright green without any sprinklers. I really like both places, but they sure are different.

Mom and I get our stuff unpacked. I'm dumping my dirty clothes into the hamper when she comes into my room. "I brought you a couple of souvenirs."

"Hey, I always wanted one of these." I hold up a T-shirt that reads MY MOTHER WENT TO CALIFORNIA AND ALL I GOT WAS THIS DUMB SHIRT. "Now the whole neighborhood will know how mean you are." I pull off my other T-shirt and put the new one on.

I know she can tell I'm joking, but she asks, "Was it that bad?"

"No," I tell her. "You got to see the ocean, and I got to see a bunch of dead people. I guess it came out about even," I say and then smile. She smiles back.

There's not much food in the house, so while my mom listens to her messages I ride my bike down to the store. I lock it into the empty rack before I go in, but when I come out a few minutes later, there are familiar bikes surrounding mine. The grocery bags I'm carrying suddenly feel heavier when I realize that Jason and Anthony are here.

I know my combination, but I fumble with the lock anyway. I open it on the second try, put one grocery bag over each handlebar, and take off toward home. Somehow it doesn't surprise me when, after a block and a half, I hear shouting behind me.

"Hey, Stan-is-lousy, long time no see!"

Grocery bags and all, I know I can out-pedal these guys, and for the first few seconds my legs act like the heroes in my escape plan. *Pump. Pump. Pump.*

Even as I pedal faster, though, I feel like I'm watching myself in a movie. The big guy is in the lead, and the yelling creeps are hot on his trail. I want the guy in front to win, but when he does I'm not sure he'll be the hero. It could be he's just a fast-pedaling coward.

Before I can decide how to rewrite the script, my legs decide to take over. I slam on my brakes and pivot my bike in a gritty cloud of dust.

I get off the bike and set the kickstand. I'm standing at full height as Jason and Anthony approach. They've both slowed down and are wearing matching looks of confusion.

"Did you say something?" I ask. I stare back and forth between them.

Jason is biting his lip and seeming nervous, but when Anthony talks, he's as cocky as ever. "I said, 'Long time no see, Stan-is-lousy.'"

"The name is Stan-is-law-ski," I say slowly. "It's a long name, but I'm sure you can remember it if you try really hard." I wrap my hand around his handlebar, giving his bike a tiny jolt. "Or you could just call me Brad."

Everybody's quiet for a minute, then Jason points to my shirt. "Your mom went to California, huh? That's cool."

I don't take my eyes off Anthony. "Yeah, it was." I drop my hand from his bike.

Jason gives Anthony a punch on the arm. "So, you ready to get out of here?"

Anthony shakes him off. "Yeah," and turns his bike around.

Jason gives me a little wave as he follows him. "Later, Brad," he says.

My mom tells me more about her vacation as she starts to get dinner ready. I still hope to visit California someday, but it can wait. Given the choice between seeing palm trees or meeting my grandfather, I know I got the better deal.

It's a nice evening, so I take my sketchpad out on the back porch. I flip past the Jason and Anthony monsters to find a clean page. I start with some muscles and broad, sturdy shoulders. Before long, I've added the face of a noble-looking hero with an intense stare. There's a breeze blowing in his hair, hair that looks like mine on a good day, but the line of his jaw is all Grandpa's. My pencil twirls and swirls until there's a trout stream running alongside the hero's gigantic sneaker.

My signature is small and professional-looking, but the title on the picture is bold. I think I'll mail it to my grandfather. I know he'll appreciate my portrait of Stanislawski the Great.

DATE DUE

GAYLORD   #3523PI   Printed in USA